D0801821

Every Day, Every Hour

Nataša Dragnić

Translated by Liesl Schillinger

VIKING

VIKING
Published by the Penguin Group
Penguin Group (USA) Inc., 375 Hudson Street, New York, New York 10014, U.S.A. •
Penguin Group (Canada), 90 Eglinton Avenue East, Suite 700, Toronto, Ontario,
Canada M4P 2Y3 (a division of Pearson Penguin Canada Inc.) • Penguin Books Ltd,
80 Strand, London WC2R 0RL, England • Penguin Ireland, 25 St. Stephen's Green,
Dublin 2, Ireland (a division of Penguin Books Ltd) • Penguin Books Australia Ltd,
250 Camberwell Road, Camberwell, Victoria 3124, Australia (a division of Pearson
Australia Group Pty Ltd) • Penguin Books India Pvt Ltd, 11 Community Centre,
Panchsheel Park, New Delhi – 110 017, India • Penguin Group (NZ), 67 Apollo Drive,
Rosedale, Auckland 0632, New Zealand (a division of Pearson NewZealand Ltd) •
Penguin Books (South Africa) (Pty) Ltd, 24 Sturdee Avenue, Rosebank, Johannesburg
2196, South Africa

Penguin Books Ltd, Registered Offices:
80 Strand, London WC2R 0RL, England

First published in 2012 by Viking Penguin,
a member of Penguin Group (USA) Inc.

10 9 8 7 6 5 4 3 2 1

Copyright © Deutsche Verlags-Anstalt, a division of Verlagsgruppe Random House
GmbH, Munchen, Germany, 2011
Translation copyright © Liesl Schillinger, 2012
All rights reserved

First published in Germany by Verlagsgruppe Random House GmbH under the title
Jeden Tag, jede Stunde.

Excerpts from *Cien sonetos de amor* and *Los versos del capitan* by Pablo Neruda. © Fundacion
Pablo Neruda, 2011. By permission of Agencia Literaria Carmen Balcells S.A.

Publisher's Note
This is a work of fiction. Names, characters, places, and incidents either are the product
of the author's imagination or are used fictitiously, and any resemblance to actual persons,
living or dead, business establishments, events, or locales is entirely coincidental.

LIBRARY OF CONGRESS CATALOGING IN PUBLICATION DATA

Dragnic, Nataša.
[Jeden tag, jede stunde. English]
Every day, every hour / Natasa Dragnic ; translated by Liesl Schillinger.
p.   cm.
ISBN 978-0-670-02350-9
1. Friendship in children—Fiction. 2. Separated people—Fiction. 3. Croatia—Fiction.
4. Paris (France)—Fiction. I. Schillinger, Liesl. II. Title.
PT2704.R34J4313 2012
833'.92—dc23   2011043715

Printed in the United States of America
Set in Adobe Caslon Pro with Basilia Com
Designed by Daniel Lagin

No part of this book may be reproduced, scanned, or distributed in any printed or
electronic form without permission. Please do not participate in or encourage piracy of
copyrighted materials in violation of the author's rights. Purchase only authorized
editions.

for B.

But
if every day,
every hour
you feel that you are destined for me . . .
oh my love, oh my own,
all that fire endures in me still,
in me nothing is extinguished or forgotten
                                          —*Pablo Neruda*

"I t's hard to believe."

"What is?"

"That I'm here."

"Why?"

"After so many years."

"It's nice."

"Like sleeping in your own bed after a long trip."

"I know."

"Like tasting something you haven't tasted since childhood."

"Those round, white lollipops."

"With the picture in the middle."

"And the colored border."

A waterfall of memories. A small hotel room in the heat of summer. Pine trees that grant rescuing shade. Too much light. When you've got secrets. When you don't want to be disturbed. When any other person is one person too many. When you feel more at ease at dusk. When you can touch every corner of the room from the bed.

"Hardly anything has changed here."

"You think?"

"I can still picture you."

"But without gray hair and without a walking stick."

"How are you?"

"The nightmares hardly come anymore."

"That's good."

"Yes."

"Why are you smiling?"

"Because I can still picture you as well."

A beautiful young woman. At the reception desk. In a tight, dark blue dress. Flat white sandals. Two big trunks. A white handbag. Fingers full of rings. Long, curly hair. Unruly. It gets in her eyes. She keeps blowing it away. Blue-white earrings. A narrow face. Full lips. A wide nose. Big, dark eyes. Impatient hands. An elegant watch.

"I forgot about my work."

"When?"

"When you came into the lobby."

"When?"

"Back then. Don't you remember?"

"I don't need to remember."

"And seeing you is . . ."

". . . like a dream."

". . . like Christmas."

"And Easter."

"And birthdays."

"And the first day of spring."

"All together."

.   .   .

Their bodies next to each other. Sweaty. Tired. Hungry. Insatiable. Happy. On damp sheets. A hand on the stomach. A fingernail on an upper arm. Mouth on breast. Leg over hip. His green eyes.

"Have you thought of me?"

"How many times, my love, did I love you without seeing you, and perhaps without memory, / without recognizing your glance, without beholding you."

"I'd almost forgotten."

"What?"

"You and your Neruda."

"I imagined . . ."

"What?"

"Life with you."

" . . ."

"Forever and ever."

"And?"

"It was full of wonder."

The tiny hotel room. Like a whole universe. Like a whole life. Without borders. Endless. Infinite. Like the depths of the ocean. Unexplored. Full of secrets. Frightening. Irresistible. Fascinating. Like the number of stars in the sky. Unknown. Unsettling. Indestructible. Immortal.

"How is your daughter?"

"I have two."

"Congratulations."

"Thank you."

"No, I thank you."

"What for?"

"Just because."

"Why?"

"Forget it."

"I don't want to forget."

"Have it your way."

"Do you have children?"

"A son."

"How old?"

"Seventeen."

"Seventeen?"

"Yes."

"I wonder . . ."

"What?"

"So, a son."

"Yes."

"I . . ."

. . . love you only you always you my whole life long you are my breath my heartbeat you are infinite in me you are the sea that I see and the fish that I catch you have lured into my net you are my day and my night and the asphalt under my shoes and the tie around my neck and the skin on my body and the bones beneath my skin and my boat and my breakfast and my wine and my friends and my morning coffee and my paintings and my paintings and my wife in my heart and my wife my wife my wife my wife . . .

"I've got to go now."

"Please don't."

"Why not?"

"It's cruel."

"What is?"

"To come, and then to go."

"I have no choice."

"A person always has a choice."

"It's ironic that you would say that."

"I was weak."

"Yes, you were."

"I've never gotten over it."

"Tough luck."

"I've never stopped loving you."

"I believe you."

"I want you to stay here."

"It's too late."

"Who has ever loved as we do?"

Once upon a time there was a little hotel by the sea, sheltered by pines from the cold north wind. Its southern wall tasted of salt and heat even in winter. Big windows and balcony doors reflected the waves. The sea wrapped itself around the small pebble beach like the night sky filled with stars. Where everything began. And there they lived, happily ever after. Where everything should end.

"Look, the clouds!"

"Do you remember?"

"And do you?"

Chapter 1

Luka enters the world with a soft, halfhearted cry then grows quiet as he feels water sluice over his skin. The year is 1959, in Makarska, a small, peaceful harbor town in Croatia. Anka, the midwife, is also a neighbor, so it didn't take her long to respond to the expectant father's panicked calls. She checks three times to make sure the baby is healthy and in good shape, and thinks, What an unusual child. She shakes her head gently. What will become of him, this baby who's as quiet and thoughtful as if he were eighty years old and had already seen the world? And yet, he's as blind as a kitten. Luka's exhausted mother, Antica, asks anxiously if everything's all right with the baby because he's not crying anymore. The midwife composes herself, and tells the mother—with whom she's drunk countless quarts of strong Turkish coffee over the years—that everything's just as it should be, that she just needs to recover, rest and gather strength for later, for her little son's sake. "What a sturdy lad he is, we'll be hearing about him someday," she says. The mother asks for her son. She wants to hold him. "He's going to be called

Luka," she says proudly and a little shyly. The midwife knows this already and nods agreement. "You can see at once that this here is a proper Luka," she says, placing the silent boy—whose eyes are wide open, as if they were his lone window onto the world—in his mother's arms. A blind kitten, she thinks again. In a moment both of them fall asleep. Mother and son. It's a warm November day. Windless and fair. A winter that is not yet winter.

Luka is three years old. His father, Zoran, takes him fishing for the first time. He has a small boat, which Luka calls his own. That always makes Zoran smile and wink at Luka's mother. Then she smiles, too. The father takes Luka's hand in his own and they go to the harbor. With his right hand, Luka holds tight to his father. In his left hand he carries a small bag that holds many colored pencils and a sketchbook. Luka loves to paint and draw. He doesn't go anywhere without this bag. Today he wants to fish more than anything. But also, to paint. On the way, they run into many people. On Kačić Square, everyone greets them, everyone knows them, everyone smiles at Luka and asks him what he's got planned. Luka can hardly speak for pride. "Going fishing," he says, too loudly, and hides his art bag behind his back. People laugh. Some of them ask with exaggerated concern if such a very little boy should be allowed to go fishing. Luka wavers between fear that he might be forbidden to go and anger that anybody would dare question his father's judgment. But his father just makes a serious face and squeezes Luka's sweaty hand. Everything's fine, no need for him to worry. They go farther. Then farther still. As they walk along the Riva, Luka walks closest to the sea and looks into the water. He greets every fish with a soft cry. And so they continue, all the way to the boat. It's not a long distance for his father. But for a three-year-old, it's a major expedition. His left hand already hurts. His bag is heavy. So many pencils! The little boat floats peacefully between other boats its size. MA 38. That's the red license number. Almost all the boats are white with a thin blue stripe around them. Or else they're completely white. Luka can already spot his father's boat. He's already been on the boat a million times. Maybe more. He's just never gone fishing. Luka loves the sea and the boat more than anything. "When I grow up, I'll be a sailor," he says. Or a fisherman. His father steps lightly into the boat. He hoists Luka high above the water and sets him down next to him. The boat isn't all that big, but it has a small cabin. Luka sits down. He watches his father as he expertly steers the boat out of the harbor. Luka will be like his father one day. They head out onto the open sea. Between the Saint Petar and Osejava peninsulas. In the distance, he can make out the stones of the Church of St. Petar, the stones that remained after the earthquake. The earthquake was awful, the whole house had trembled, and Mom had cried, and Dad had taken them all to the basement, and it had lasted a long time, longer than anything Luka could think of, and he had been scared, very scared, but they had made it through all right, and nothing much had happened, except that his stuffed animals got all jumbled, Dad had seen to everything—and then his father turns off the motor. The boat drifts in the water. "What's the name of that island over there?" his father asks. Luka likes this game. He's good at it. "Brač." Luka's voice wavers, though he knows he's got the right answer. "Good. And over there?" "Far," Luka says quickly. His father smiles. "Yes, almost right. Hvar. That's a hard word, sometimes I don't pronounce it right myself." Luka grows pensive. He hopes he hasn't ruined everything. But his father is holding a fishing rod. So everything's okay. Luka swallows with excitement. He leans over the edge of the boat looking for fish, and calls out to them that they'd better hurry up and get ready, because he's coming. He dips his little hand into the sea. "Here, here, little fishy," he whispers. Then he raises his glance and meets his father's eyes. Today is the best day of my life, Luka thinks, and closes his eyes. Sea creatures nibble on his fingers.

While Luka's hand teases fish in the sea, Dora enters the world with a cry so shrill that it makes Anka, the midwife, burst out laughing. It's the delivery room of the Franciscan Cloister Hospital, the year is 1962. Such a strong, vigorous girl, Anka says. The exhausted mother, Helena, can say nothing. She can't even smile. She can only think to herself that, at last, it's over. Finally. It's the first and last child she'll have, she thinks. She closes her eyes and falls asleep. Dora's loud cries don't rouse her. The midwife marvels at the vitality of the tiny creature. She looks at her lovingly. She strokes her little head and her trembling little body. The midwife is old—though, of course, compared to this little creature, anyone is old—and has had much experience. She has delivered countless children. She's seen them all. But this little girl! The baby's tireless, deafening wails pierce her heart, with faultless aim. Not once do they miss their mark. No detour. Quiet tears fill the midwife's eyes. She has no children of her own. She never married. Her fiancé died in the war. Shot by Italians. After that, there were no other men in her life. That's how it was back then. And now, since the big earthquake in January, which left only the west wall of her cottage standing, she's had to move in with her younger sister, and put up with her sister's husband, who gets drunk too often, and likes to make jokes about her single life. Nasty, coarse jokes. She curls her index finger and touches the baby's small round mouth with her knuckle. Surprised and distracted, the baby falls quiet. Her nearly blind eyes find the midwife, catch her gaze and hold it. She will be called Dora, but everybody knows that already.

Dora is two years old and a lively girl. Her mother says she's a wild thing. Dora doesn't understand why, not that it bothers her. Because her mother smiles when she says it. And her father sets her on his shoulders and runs around with her like he's her horsey. "When Dora laughs, the whole city shakes," her mother says. At two, Dora talks like no other baby. As if she were five already. "And she understands everything, too," her mother says, not without pride. Dora can never have enough. She has to touch everything, see everything, go everywhere. In town, on Kalalarga Street, along the Riva, by the waterfront or on Kačić Square, she calls out to the people hurrying past, and the ones who stop, forgetting their hurry, smile at her uncertainly and curiously, and say hello or answer her questions. Dora is very sure-footed, she never falls, she never runs, she just walks very quickly. She takes big steps, and it can be strange, and sometimes even a little funny, to watch her speed along. Dora never jumps either. She steps down from a wall with one giant airborne stride. "Are you afraid?" her mother asks. Dora avoids her mother's gaze and doesn't answer. And doesn't jump.

Luka is five years old when he gets a sister. Her name is Ana and she's tiny and cries a lot. His mother can barely get back on her feet, and his father works more than he used to, and Luka sees less and less of him, and he feels an overpowering urge to paint, the whole house fills up with his paintings. Now he goes to kindergarten, even though his mother doesn't work, and the other kids are sometimes so mean to him that he goes into the bathroom and cries and paints where nobody can see him, including Aunt Vera, who looks after all the children, but likes him best of all. She often runs her hand through his hair, gives him a warm smile or a wink and reads his favorite story aloud, over and over, even though the other children whine that the story is boring and that they already know it by heart. Really, though, Luka wishes he could stay in kindergarten all day long and never go home, where his stupid little sister is always crying, and Mom's always tired, and Dad isn't there, and Luka is always on the verge of sobbing, though he stifles it and nobody notices. He's unhappy all the same, and he wishes everything could be the way it used to be, when his father would take him fishing and they would go out on the boat and he would get to paint and catch fish and his father would ask him riddles that were funny and sometimes kind of tricky; like, for instance, if a white cow gives white milk, what kind of milk does a black cow give? Which obviously is not an easy question at all, but he knew all the answers. And sometimes they would stay out until after sundown, but they always, always had so much fun together.

Dora understands. Her mother speaks clearly and slowly and is sad, and Dora understands. But Dora isn't sad that, at the age of two, she will have to start going to kindergarten three times a week, because Mom has to start working again, and Dora doesn't have grandparents nearby to look after her. Her grandparents live far, far away. Dora has visited them many times already. In a big city. "It's the capital, pure and simple," Mom says, then Dad gets annoyed and corrects her. Belgrade is the capital, Zagreb is just a big city. The president lives in Belgrade. Mom murmurs something under her breath. Dora can tell she's not happy. It's not because of the president; everyone likes him, he's always surrounded by children and flowers. It's the city he lives in that Mom's not happy about. So when she's alone again with Mom, Dora tells her, We'll drive to Grandma and Grandpa's, in the capital. And Mom smiles and quickly looks over her shoulder. Zagreb. They had to drive a long time in the car to get there. So long that Dora fell asleep many times along the way. Dora remembers everything. Her head is full of pictures that speak, that have a scent, that sometimes also have a taste. And she can put it all into words. "What a memory the girl has!" her mother says, as if she could scarcely believe it. "Like an elephant," her father agrees, marveling. A peculiar child, some think, but don't say. Dora gives the matter no thought. Sometimes she stands a long time in front of the mirror and stares at herself, at her face that is capable of changing so quickly, as if she had a hundred faces, she likes doing that. That's the way she is. Every face she sees in the mirror is her. And she's looking forward to meeting the children in kindergarten, whom she doesn't yet know. And she's also looking forward to the toys. She's not afraid. "For Dora, life is an adventure," her mother always says, raising her eyebrows, which looks really silly and makes Dora laugh. And Dad reads the paper.

Luka sees the new girl who's just come in. She has black hair, long and wavy. And shiny. Like a fish's bright scales. She's small and thin and quick, and younger than all the other kids in kindergarten, and he can't take his eyes off her. The girl's mother carries her bag, which has white and blue stripes. With a big yellow fish in the middle. He likes it a lot, this bag. Even though he doesn't recognize the kind of fish. He has a black backpack that he didn't get to choose for himself, which he once attacked with scissors, hoping that he would then be given a new one, but that didn't work, it just became even more horrible. Now the backpack is ugly *and* damaged. So he stuffs it in a plastic bag and carries the bag around with him. And nobody notices. If only he had a cool bag like the new girl's. Luka can see himself walking around with this superbag, with his paints and sketchbook inside it, admired and envied by everyone. Proudly he would cross Kačić Square, and slowly stride to the Marineta, where all the people would gather to look at him and his new superbag. Nobody would be able to take their eyes off him. Maybe then Mom would smile again and give Dad a kiss like she used to, and say his name softly, many times over, like she used to—Zoran, Zoran, Zoran, Luka can almost hear it—and then Dad would beam with pleasure and take Luka fishing with him. Yes, for sure he would, and then he'd give him really tough riddles, like, for example, if Mom and Dad are white, but their child is born in Africa, what color skin will the kid have, which is a hard question, but that wouldn't matter, because he'd know all the answers. If only he had a bag like that. Like the new girl's. He can't take his eyes off her!

Dora enters the kindergarten room expectantly and looks around her. A tall boy is standing by the bookshelf, staring at her. This doesn't faze her. She takes off her jacket. She doesn't want Mom to help her as long as the tall boy is watching. Maybe that's how it is in kindergarten. Maybe one kid will always be standing around the whole day long staring at the other kids, maybe it's some kind of neat game. Dora can hardly wait to get to play it. She wants to take her shoes off by herself, too. "What's gotten into you, Dorrie?" Mom wonders. Mom doesn't get it. She doesn't know that Dora is playing a really neat new game, and that the boy is staring Dora down, and that she's supposed to be brave and stare right back at him if she wants to stay in the game, and she absolutely wants to be the one who gets to stand, immobile, by the shelf filled with picture books, staring everybody down, like he's doing, oh yes, she wants that, no matter what. So Dora shakes her head and says nothing. Because her head suddenly starts to swim. It feels full and hollow and blown up like a balloon, and hot and light and fluttery and transparent. She closes her eyes. She has no shoe on her left foot. She sits on the floor as if she were in a trance. "What's wrong with you, sweetie?" her mother asks again. Dora looks at her. In a moment Mom will start crying. My sweetheart, my Dorrie!

Luka doesn't move. He leans against the bookshelf and holds his breath. He's afraid that if he relaxes his muscles and breathes, the bag will disappear. He fixates on the bag until it hurts, and his eyes begin tearing up. He counts: one, two, three, four, five, six, seven . . . and then the world around him melts away and he slides to the floor. Everything around him is quiet. Little by little he slips away. Like pictures in a book whose pages he slowly flips through.

Dora is the first to come to the side of the boy who fainted. She crouches beside him, tinier than tiny. Her eyes widen, until her face, paler than pale, seems to be nothing but eyes. She bends her head over the boy, and, before the woman who is now kneeling at the boy's other side, raising his legs, can stop her or send her away, Dora kisses him, on his pale red mouth. "Dora!" her mother calls out in shock. No time for pet names.

Luka hears a soft voice next to his face. "You are my sleeping beauty, only mine, wake up, my prince, you are my prince, only mine . . ."

Then other voices and words reach his ears, until, confused and weak, he opens his eyes and . . .

. . . she sees his eyes, opening slowly, his confused expression, his lips that move without making a sound . . .

. . . but he can say nothing, so he smiles faintly and . . .

. . . she smiles, too, and . . .

. . . he shakily raises his arm, stretches his hand toward her face, touches her long, black hair, and asks himself where the bag might have gotten to, wonders if maybe he could persuade her to give it to him, as a present, to cheer him up, and . . .

. . . she whispers once again very softly, so softly that only her lips move: "My prince, only mine."

Chapter 2

"**D**o you see it there, the really little one, like a scoop of ice cream?"

Dora points with her outstretched arm. A round lollipop sticks out between her sticky fingers. She points high up in the sky, and even though their heads are very close to each other, Luka can't see the cloud scoop.

They're stretched out on the roof of the cabin of his father's boat, looking up at the clouds that a light summer breeze is nudging across the sky. It's early afternoon and a stillness has fallen over the harbor. Every now and then a tourist passes. The locals are hiding out from the burning sun, their shutters drawn. Everyone seeks out the deepest shade and tries not to move. In heat like this, it's sometimes hard just to breathe.

Only the tourists don't seem to figure this out. They walk around all day without hats and end up in the emergency room. Luka knows this well. He sees them on the beach every morning, close to the Yellow House and near to where he earns his pocket money by renting out beach umbrellas. He's nine years old. He's good-looking. Dora says so, too. He's let his hair grow, and it glints in the sun as if it were full of glitter. His skin, usually pale, has taken on a deep cocoa tone. At home, Luka often looks at his body in the mirror. He doesn't like what he sees that much; he's too skinny. But that will change soon, because in May he joined the water polo team. Every morning he gets up at seven, wolfs down a slice of bread, and runs to practice. Seagull, the club is called. His father used to play water polo there. A long time ago, of course. Before Luka was born. Mom saw him there and fell in love with him. All the girls fall in love with water polo players; it's obvious why. They're tall and strong and, basically, great guys. Better than soccer players. He's happy about that. About the water and his friends and his muscles. If only it wasn't all going to end in September. Stupid September! And Dora. He can't think about that. About September and Dora in the same breath. He can't. No way.

Dora comes to the beach every morning at the same time he does. Unless she has watched him at practice. She does that a lot. She lays her towel next to his folding chair, watches him paint, goes swimming with him when he takes a break, and stays till lunchtime. Then they leave together to go to their houses, stopping to buy an ice cream at the dairy if one of them has some money. The dairy is the only place in Makarska where you can get ice cream, and there's always a line. Dora always gets chocolate, of course—for her chocolate is the only flavor on earth—and he gets lemon, he likes the tart, bitter taste. It refreshes him, and it lingers so long on his tongue, sometimes even until after lunch. They part only at the last little crossing, where Dora runs up a steep, tiny hill and Luka makes a right turn, then two lefts. Since they're hungry only when they're together, at home they poke sullenly at their plates, push the food back and forth and gulp down whole mouthfuls without properly chewing them. Their mothers complain, wonder what's wrong, get worried, tease them, shout at them, threaten, ask if they're feeling well, lay their hands on their foreheads, look at them with concern, cook their favorite foods, despair and shrug their shoulders. Then the table is cleared and everyone goes back to their bedrooms to wait out the unbearable heat of the afternoon and to rest—which the kids ought to do, too.

Instead, Dora and Luka always sneak back outside, every day, all summer long, while their parents nap in their bedrooms. For them, napping would be a huge waste of the valuable time they have left to spend in each other's company—as is any moment they don't share together.

"Do you see it or don't you?" Dora's voice has already grown a little impatient. "You can't say you see something if you don't!" She plays with her hair. Like she always does.

Luka keeps quiet. He's thinking about September, and he doesn't want to talk. He turns and looks at Dora beside him, observing her concentration as she watches the clouds. He's done this for months. For years. If he were to go blind it wouldn't matter, he already knows her face inside out.

"It doesn't count. The only clouds that count are the ones you've actually seen." She breathes excitedly and her eyelids start fluttering. "So, now what? If you don't see it, I've won! Because you didn't see the one before it either, even though it was so clear. It couldn't have been anything but a flying coach with a pigeon on the roof. It was easy to see. But you didn't see it . . ." She gasps. After a little pause she asks quietly: "Or don't you want to play with me anymore?"

A boat leaves the harbor. The motor drones loudly. The sea swells almost imperceptibly, but enough to gently rock Dora and Luka on the boat's roof. Their bodies touch softly, separate, touch, separate, touch . . .

"I see everything, I also saw the pigeon, I just want you to win. Otherwise you're really sad, and I don't like it."

"That's not true."

"I don't like it when you're sad, I don't like it at all."

Luka is still lying on his side, watching Dora's face. Don't think about it, he tells himself, don't think about the fact that this face will soon be gone.

Dora says nothing for a while. Then she sits up and clutches her knees.

"I am *not* sad. That's not true. I'm not sad when I don't win. It's mean to say something that isn't true. Ask anyone you want. It's mean to say something that totally isn't true. Anyone will tell you, just ask them."

She rests her forehead on her knees.

Luka can't look at her any longer. His heart beats loudly and irregularly. He feels lightheaded. He sits up, too. He doesn't dare to breathe. He closes his eyes and counts: one, two, three, four . . .

"Stop that right now! Breathe! Or you'll faint again!"

Dora shakes him so fiercely that he teeters and almost falls into the sea. He opens his eyes. Dora's face is very near, her dark eyes as big as the two pizza plates he'd seen not long before, in a restaurant on the plaza. They were so big that the waiters could hardly carry them. They wobbled in their hands, and Luka had thought the pizzas might slide onto the floor. Unfortunately, that hadn't happened.

"Let's go swimming," he says all of a sudden, and stands up. He jumps from the cabin roof to the gangplank, and from there to the shore. Without waiting for Dora, he takes long strides in the direction of Saint Petar. To the rock. Soon he hears her behind him. He smiles. She's so light, like the clouds. A wonderful image forms in his head.

"And I *did* see the cloud, but it wasn't a scoop of ice cream, nothing that dumb. It was a soccer ball, with the air let out of it."

It's been four years since Dora came to kindergarten for the first time and Luka fainted. It's been four years since Dora and Luka became inseparable. Nobody seems surprised by their friendship. Nobody questions it. Everyone looks on with interest, because the town of Makarska has never seen anything like this before. But nobody laughs either. Even the other children don't laugh. Not once. They play with Dora and Luka or they leave them alone. There's something strange in the air when Dora and Luka are together. You can't call it calm, and you can't call it storm. It smells of mandarin oranges and roasted almonds, of the sea and fresh-baked cookies, and springtime. As if they were enveloped in a cloud. Some people say the cloud is turquoise, others that it's orange. Domica, the old woman who sits in front of her house on the edge of the woods between the Riva and the beach, says the cloud is light blue, nearly as pale as the sky in summer. Then she nods knowingly and closes her half-blind eyes. Ever since Domica predicted the earthquake six years ago, the townspeople have been a little fearful of her, but they still come to her for advice. Especially young women in love.

For some reason, Luka's and Dora's parents also don't find it unusual that a two-year-old and a five-year-old would become friends. And what friends! Now and then, seeing their children at play, they look at each other thoughtfully, as if remembering something best forgotten. On such occasions, you might catch them smiling distract-edly, lost in a daydream. But they never raise an objection, and they do everything possible to let the children see each other every day, even outside of kindergarten. And when Luka entered the kindergar-ten classroom one day holding Dora's bag, and she came in with his battered backpack, hardly anyone noticed. And nobody thought to ask what had become of the old plastic bag.

Luka's four-year-old sister, Ana, also wants to play with them or go places with them, which usually doesn't suit Luka and Dora. But sometimes, especially in summer, during the long school vacation, Luka has to take her with him, his mother says so, he can't get out of it. Then the three of them sit around his beach umbrella and throw stones into the sea, but Dora and Luka never, ever take her with them to visit their rock! The rock on the Saint Petar peninsula belongs only to them, to them alone, and a meddling sister or any other kid has no business there. That's clear. Dora and Luka don't even have to talk about it, don't even need to exchange a conspiratorial glance, not even once. They will go with Ana to get ice cream. That's okay. An ice cream cone, that's nothing special. Or they'll play "catch the ball" with her in shallow water, or see who can find the thickest tree. Or share a soda, if they're all thirsty. That's fine. But the rock? Not a chance. And there's something else that belongs only to the two of them as well: the clouds. The clouds above, in the sky that belongs to everyone.

Ana likes Dora. She wants Dora to be her friend. At kindergarten, she's already told everyone that Dora is, in fact, her best friend. Everyone is jealous of her. Everyone knows Dora. Even the ones she doesn't know have heard about her. Dora is funny and tells great stories, it's never boring when she's around, she has an answer for everything. And she's got her own bike, which is red and shiny and darts around in the sunshine like a giant flame. Ana wants one, too. When Ana tells Luka this, he just laughs and walks away, as if to say, nobody can be like Dora. Or ride a bike like Dora. Sometimes Ana thinks that Dora lives in a fairy tale, and that she's a princess in disguise, only here among the rest of them on a visit. Ana loves fairy tales. Sometimes Dora reads stories to her; sometimes she tells them to her. Other times, she makes up new stories, and acts them out for her. Ana likes that best of all. Then Dora transforms herself into a damsel in distress, an evil queen, a fire-breathing dragon, a crying king, a brave prince, a good fairy, a wicked witch. One after the other. Or all of them at the same time. It's more exciting than the movies. Yes, Ana likes Dora. Above all, because Dora shared a secret with her. She showed her how a person can make faces in a mirror and become anyone and anything. You could even make faces with no story attached, just because you felt like it: Dora calls this an "important exercise." She collects film magazines and knows everything about all the actors. Some days, she lets Ana touch the pictures of the famous actors, but only briefly, fleetingly, while she counts to five. Ana is grateful to Dora, but thinks all the same that she's too strict. What could happen? They're just photographs! "I'll be like that one day," Dora sometimes whispers, and Ana doesn't exactly understand what she means: Will she be that pretty, that untouchable, that full of secrets, or that black-and-white?

Dora likes Ana, too. She's Luka's sister, after all, and Dora likes everything that she shares with Luka. It's also obvious who matters more to him. Luka strung together the shell necklace for her—for Dora, and for no one else. Only Luka held Dora's hand in a way that made her heart beat faster and her mouth water. Only with Luka does she share her favorite lollipop, the round, white kind, with the colored border and the picture in the middle. She doesn't find it disgusting to lick the lollipop after Luka has put it in his mouth. The same way that her mother doesn't mind eating with Dora's fork, or drinking from her glass. "That's how mothers are," Mom would say, and smile. Dora asks herself why she feels the same way about Luka, even though she's not his mother. She's a hundred percent not his mother. It would be truly weird for a mother to be younger than her child! One time, Dora even brushed her teeth with Luka's toothbrush. Anyway, Dora would like to have a sister or a brother of her own. She would like to have someone soft and cuddly and adorable to play with. Her mom tells her she'd be better off with a dog or a cat. But Dora doesn't want that. She's a little afraid of cats. Just a very little, of course, because Dora really is afraid of nothing. Like that girl overseas somewhere she'd heard about, who felt completely fine, but was actually terribly sick. Doctors found out she had internal bleeding throughout her body, even though she had no symptoms. The difference, though, is that Dora isn't sick. Not at all. She's never been sick in her life. She's simply fearless. "Pure and simple," her mother would say. Mom says that a lot: "pure and simple." It's practically a code word with her, an identifying mark—like the seven baby goats who can recognize their mother by her white foot. Dora thinks it's hilarious how many times a day her mother says it—making big eyes and shaking her head for emphasis. Some days, Dora keeps a tally. Dora likes her mother. And Luka. But she's aware that she likes them in different ways. Dora understood early on that there are different ways, and different kinds, of liking. Pure and simple.

And Luka likes Dora. He thinks everything about her is fantastic.

He often wishes she were his sister, so they could be together all the time, day and night. It would be cool to have a sister like that. Or maybe not. Sometimes Luka feels uneasy, he has a feeling, or a bunch of feelings, that he can't pin down, that frighten him. When they overtake him, he's relieved that he can run home, where there's no Dora, and everything is straightforward and familiar and easy. Then he lies awake in bed and tries to think of something besides Dora, but it's no use. She's always on his mind; he sees her small face, her big eyes, hears her laughing and telling stories—she never runs out of stories— and before long he starts missing her, gets up, runs out of the house and goes looking for her. He always finds her. The two of them like to sneak into the hospital that's in the cloister, a kind of church, because Dora likes the smell of the place, and the high ceiling in the waiting room. They take a seat, and pretend they're waiting for a doctor, or for their parents, but everyone knows who they are, and after they smile at them, they generally leave them alone. Because they always greet them politely. Once Dora showed Luka the room where she was born. She shares everything with him. Like a real girlfriend, even.

"Wait for me!"

She can't keep up with him, he hears her steps behind him, she's tagging after him. Like a puppy. Dora still won't run. She just refuses to, and Luka can't persuade her. It's a mystery to him why she won't. Dora is a mystery to him, too, though he doesn't know anybody better than he knows her. He knows everything about her. Everything. What he hasn't personally witnessed in her company, she tells him. What she doesn't tell him, he senses. Dora is a part of him, like his leg or his hair. His lungs. And that's why he can't bear to think about

September. Then life will suddenly stop making sense. He's afraid he'll forget how to breathe.

"Wait for me!"

Dora hurries. But she has no hope of keeping up with Luka. The rocks crunch under her feet. Her eyes start to burn. She forbids herself to cry. She invents imaginary punishments for herself if she sheds even one tear. She will never again eat ice cream. Or chocolate. Or go with Luka to Partizan, the outdoor summer theater—which would be a pity, because there are good movies coming up that she absolutely has to see. With her favorite actress, Elizabeth Taylor. She's the most beautiful woman in the world! Or she will never again let herself read a good book. Or . . .

"Why are you crying?"

Luka always gets terrified when Dora cries. He's sweating. He wipes his naked forearm over his forehead. Everything is sticky. His glance travels over Dora from head to foot. Only a few steps separate them from the rock. The lighthouse is right behind them. Nobody else is around. All they can hear is the sea.

"I'm not crying at all."

But Luka can clearly, distinctly, see her tears.

"You are, too!"

"I am not!"

They shriek at each other like two fighting little birds. Dora crosses her arms and glares at him with an angry, injured look. Luka's arms hang beside his gangly frame. He has only one goal, which is not to think.

"Why are your eyes so wet, then?"

"They're not!"

"Yes they are, they're terribly wet, wetter than I am after water polo practice."

"You're lying, you're lying! It's just sweat!" And she rubs her face with both hands, incessantly, her hands moving faster and faster, harder and harder . . .

"Be careful, you'll hurt yourself!"

Luka tries to hold her hands still, but she won't let him, she fights as if for her life. And then all at once, she stops. As if she'd turned to stone. Luka feels like he's about to stop breathing. He starts counting in his head. Nobody can hear him, he's sure of it. He's pressed his lips together so tightly that no sound can slip out. He's even remembered to keep his eyes open. Nothing will give him away.

"You're going to faint again!" Dora jabs him in the stomach and quickly runs off, toward the rock.

Luka opens his eyes—so he *had* closed them! how dumb of him!—and follows her. Right before she reaches the rock, he takes her hand—it's hot and sweaty and slippery—in his and holds it tightly. He doesn't have giant muscles yet, his water polo training hasn't yet become evident in his body. But all the same, his grip is strong and unyielding.

Dora comes to a stop. All by herself. Luka has nothing to with it. But they're already there. Above their rock. In the heat of the early afternoon sun. Out of breath.

"Maybe we should go out on the boat instead!"

Luka's voice is faint. He's holding Dora's hand. He's standing on a big, fairly jagged ledge, but he imagines he's on the boat, riding the waves, with Dora next to him, clinging to the edge of the cabin as if she were afraid of falling into the sea. He grins. Naturally, she would never let on that she was afraid, never. But he knows better. It's not that she's afraid of the water, she just doesn't want to fall in.

They've gone out many times on his father's boat; they're allowed to, as long as they keep near the coast and don't stay out longer than an hour. To Bratuš and back. Or to Tučepi and back. Luka knows his father's boat as well as Dora knows her bicycle. He's a master captain.

"I don't want to."

But she has nothing against it. Luka knows that. She loves being on the boat, alone with Luka, on a genuine adventure. Beneath her, the sea and all the fish and the unknown depths. Above her, the sky with all its clouds, each of them with its own exciting story to tell, if you listen right. You've got to keep your eyes open, but not totally open, you draw your eyelids together a little, into slits. Then you can see everything more distinctly.

"Why not?" Luka doesn't understand. Normally she always wants to go out on the boat. He remembers the first time. That first time, they were allowed to go only as far as Osejava, while his father and Dora's mother waited for them in the harbor—they hadn't let them out of their sight the entire time. They'd had fun just the same, and laughed when Dora tried to imitate a dolphin—the way they duck their heads and leap—and nearly fell into the water. They'd only ever seen dolphins in pictures. Luka likes dolphins, he would love to see one for real. "You would die from fright, you would think it was a shark," Dora had told him, laughing, and almost fell into the water all over again. But she's a good swimmer. Both of them are good swimmers. They're like fish, his mother says. Luka's mother isn't overly fond of the sea herself. Having spent half of her life "up in the mountains," she never really learned to swim well, and she's afraid of the water. When she has to go in, she only wades where it's shallow. "Better safe than sorry," she says at such times, eyeing his father mistrustfully. Luka's dad laughs then, and kisses her, or at least he used to; these days he hardly laughs anymore, and kisses her more rarely still. But Luka doesn't want to think about that now. It's too much, with September looming, and Dora not wanting to go out on the boat anymore. It's altogether too much to think about. He doesn't know what to do. He's just turned nine years old, and he doesn't even have one season of water polo under his belt!

"I want to go down to the rock," she says petulantly, but her face has a faraway look, as if just torn from sleep.

"Suit yourself." But a voice inside his head shouts, You don't have much more time. Soon everything will be over, and we won't be able to go out on the waves in my boat. He conjures the wildest scenes, hair-raising adventures that never happened and never will, far too dangerous and totally impossible, and then he starts to feel like counting again.

The rock is high and steep and bleak. But before it drops off into the sea, it extends a small plateau, a gentle lip smoothed by waves. You can lie out on the plateau, assuming you can figure out how to get down there. That is, if you know the way. Not only is the rock steep, but it cuts away at an angle, so you can't see the plateau from above. The existence of the plateau is a secret, Dora's and Luka's secret. The year before, they'd found a way to the sea through an overgrown path on a neighboring cliff, which connected to a narrow, dark, spooky tunnel that let out onto the plateau. It was Dora who found the path, and the tunnel. The surface of the plateau is smooth, and soft enough to lie on without a towel. A small, round pine grows from the rock above it. Just so. From the rock. As if from nothing. Along the descending slope of the rock, just at the spot where it meets the plateau, is a small, uncomfortable cave. They use it as a hiding place where they can dodge the rain, or keep out of the hot sun in summer, when the sun hangs high in the sky. The hiding place is higher than the end of the plateau, so the waves can't reach it. When Dora and Luka aren't there, crabs, ants and tiny translucent deep-sea creatures invade the cave and die there; and whenever Dora and Luka return, they find the remains and fling them into the sea. This spring, a swallow built her nest in the dwarf pine. Luka made a painting of the fledgling family, and gave it to Dora. Without her having to ask him. Which she would have done anyway, if he hadn't thought of it. The rock is their own, shared, private home, looking out on the islands of Brač and Hvar. It has no nameplate, no doorbell, no door. But it is their home, all the same. Clear as day.

"I wasn't crying."

"Let's go swimming."

On the water's surface, wavelets shimmer like strands of pearls.

"I've got something for you, look." Dora holds out a hand smudged with chocolate.

"What is it?"

"Chocolate. It's called a Mozartkugel. A lady in the hotel gave it to me when I brought her newspaper. It's delicious."

"How do you know? Maybe it's poisoned!"

"Why would it be poisoned? You're just jealous," Dora says, a little woefully, and looks at the ever-diminishing chocolate melting in her hand. "You've never tasted anything so good."

"I don't want it. You can't just eat everything that strangers give you."

"I know. But I know the lady. She came here last year. We're friends."

Luka can hear tears in her voice again. He turns around and runs toward the rock, before she can see him roll his eyes. "It's all the same to me. Then I'll go swimming on my own, and you can eat Mozart-kugeln with your best friend! What a stupid name!"

"Okay, I will! Then I'll go diving with her, you jerk!"

She hurries after him. All the way to the rock. Once she's there, she sits down on the dusty path and begins to unwrap the fancy paper around the chocolate. The candy has lost its shape in the heat. That doesn't bother Dora. She pops it in her mouth and licks the place on her hand where the chocolate had been.

Luka watches her. Stares at the dark brown smudge on her hand. Then he turns around rapidly and keeps going. He hurries, goes too fast, not cautiously enough, he could easily lose his footing, but he doesn't care. He's got to get as far away as possible from the brown smudge on Dora's hand.

"What are you doing? You're going to fall down!" Dora gets up and hurries after him. She keeps talking nonstop. "Do you want to break your neck and fall into the water? Then I'll have to fish you out, and if you're dead and just stuck lying there, then tomorrow I'll have to go to the seashell museum all by myself, and then who will be there for me to show things to and explain everything to, if you're dead and I have to fish your corpse up out of the sea, what will I tell your father or your mother when they say it's my fault, and that I should have taken better care of you?"

And then it happens. Luka shouts, and at almost the same time, Dora shouts, too, because she can't see Luka anymore. She rushes toward him, almost breaking her own neck, and then she sees him.

Luka is standing on the plateau—counting, she's sure—though his back is turned to her. She's furious, so furious, she's so fed up with always having to look after him that she hurls herself at him and blindly starts hitting him.

"You've got to stop it right now, just stop it, I . . ."

And then she sees it, too. And she screams. She turns her head to the side, buries it in Luka's shoulder, which is too bony, his shoulder blades dig into her face and hurt her, but she's happy for the pain, it's a welcome distraction. Anything is better than thinking about what she's just seen. She's going to be sick. She can feel it.

"What do we do now?"

Dora is trying to keep down the roast veal, the salted potatoes and the chard, the tomatoes, cucumbers and lettuce, the chocolate ice cream and the Mozartkugel, all of them trapped in her stomach, trying to get out. She doesn't trust herself to open her mouth.

"Dora, what do we do now?"

Luka looks at her in astonishment, his eyes are distressingly wide. But he's still breathing, so Dora can turn her glance away from him. She forces herself to look at the dead seagulls. First she'll just look with one eye. That's her plan. When that eye gets used to it, she'll try with both. It's not an easy thing to do! She squints, alternating the left eye with the right eye. She can do it, she's practiced it. A good actress has to know how.

"What are you doing?"

"I'm figuring out what to do," Dora lies, but only a little, because she is at least trying to figure out what to do, even if there's no easy answer.

"Do you think someone shot them? That's against the law! And why did it have to be on our rock?! They shouldn't have done it, it's our rock, they had no right . . ."

"Shut up! I can't think!" Dora looks at him furiously. "Whatever happened, whoever did it, it's our responsibility now. The birds belong to us now. They're lying on our doorstep."

Luka ponders. "You mean, like babies that people leave in front of the church in a basket, so other people will take care of them?"

"Yes, that's exactly what I mean."

Dora is proud of Luka.

"So, what do we do with them?"

"We bury them, obviously. Up in the woods."

"Do you think someone shot them?"

"No. I think they were fighting."

"Fighting? Over what?"

"Over a female seagull, of course! And in the fight, they lost their lives."

"I think that's stupid."

Luka can't believe it.

"It's romantic." Dora's voice is dreamy. "To love someone so much that you'd do anything for them . . ." She smiles as if she were in another place. As if she knew a secret that Luka would have to strain to understand. Luka doesn't like the feeling.

"That's crazy," he says, and approaches the dead gulls. He takes off his T-shirt and wraps them in it. His hands are shaking. But he wants to show that he's definitely not afraid. "So, let's go."

It's the last day of August 1968.

Chapter 3

There are conversations between children and adults in which children seem to register every single word. They nod, unperturbed, with their little heads full of curls. They don't say a word, but smile as if they understand everything completely. The parents keep blithely talking, choosing their words with care. For days they've been thinking about how and when to break the news, how to explain it. The process can go on for hours. Until they run out of words, and hit a silence. It's a silence that at first doesn't seem to portend anything terrible—as in a horror film that has no ominous score to give anything away. Like unsuspecting audience members, the parents have the deceptively reassuring illusion that everything is under control. Like sitting safe and dry inside a house during a storm, holding a glass of wine, a mug of cocoa, or a cup of tea, looking out the window at the rush and roar of the wind, the sea and the rain. Not even worrying about the shuddering of the house. When the world outside and the world inside have nothing to do with each other. Congratulating yourself on the wise decision to stay in, rather than go out with friends. Patting yourself on the back, thinking about how to make fun of them the next day. In just the same way, the grown-ups stand smiling by the window and wait, not expecting anything really.

That's when the eerie, spine-tingling music breaks in, taking them by surprise, when the children open their mouths and start asking the first serious, troubling question, and the grown-ups' house goes tumbling into the sky. And there's no rainbow in sight. And no ruby slippers. And no Wicked Witch is dead. Neither of the East nor of the West.

It's the middle of September. And Dora is hearing the answers today, not for the first time. The questions she asks are ones she's asked before. She'd already understood everything. And nothing. The words had been there for three months. But they were so painful that she'd run away from them. In the middle of June, she'd gone off to find Luka, who was painting by his umbrella, the school year had just ended, and she'd sat beside his folding chair and cried wordlessly. Luka had bought her a chocolate ice cream at the dairy, and afterward, after she'd eaten her ice cream and wiped her mouth, he'd painted a portrait of her for the first time, and she'd forgotten everything. Until the next time. After he'd finished the portrait, she'd pointed with her finger at the sky.

"Do you see, there's a cocker spaniel wagging his tail, do you see?"

Luka lies on the smooth stone beneath their rock, his legs dangling in the water. He's waiting for Dora. His sketchbook and his pencils are beside him. Above him are clouds. He doesn't want to look at them. That's a two-person game. He takes great care to forget about the smooth stone underneath him. The dead seagulls. He tries to think as little about them as he thinks about the dead crabs and beetles that he and Dora have always thrown into the sea—a kind of spring cleaning that goes on the whole year round.

Dora lies on the bed that's still hers in the room that's still hers and buries her head in the pillow that's still hers. This time she's fled only to the room that's still hers. As if she'd been afraid she wouldn't have the strength to make it to the beach, not to mention the rock. The cupboards are bare. The closet is almost empty. Her books are in boxes. The boxes are in the garage. Her collection of oddly shaped rocks is also in a box. Another box. And that box, too, is already in the garage. The pictures. The dried pine and cypress branches. The seashell necklaces that Luka made for her. The painted glass. The dolls. Everything is gone. Her sheets are still on the bed. They're a wavy blue-green color. Like the sea in the place where she went diving with Luka last summer. She wasn't afraid then, she saw admiration in Luka's eyes. She took his hand and pulled him down after her, deeper and deeper. Her heart nearly burst from joy and bliss and the rare sensation of perfection. Dora had read about such sensations before. She reads a lot, her favorite book is *Train in the Snow*. She likes the author, Mato Lovrak, and has read all his books. When she's caught up in a book, she's overcome by a feeling of fulfillment, the kind of perfection that completely envelops and satisfies her, like when she gets to eat an entire bowl of chocolate pudding all by herself, or when she lies in the bathtub in winter in really hot water, and listens to a record with her eyes closed—she's got all the fairy tales on records!—or like the time, long ago, when she found the incredible rock shaped like a butterfly going crazy. She gave it to Luka, even though he doesn't collect rocks. He put it in a glass box and set it on his nightstand, next to a picture of him and Dora on their rock, with a white, fluffy cloud behind them. "A dolphin!" she had cried. "No, a goalie, just about to jump," he had said. Dora smiles at the recollection. How can anybody be so wrong? Sunk in the pillow that's still hers, she marvels at Luka, and doesn't notice that her pillow keeps on getting wetter.

Luka lies on the smooth rock, his legs dangling in the water. He's waiting for Dora. His sketchbook and his pencils are beside him. The sun already hangs low over the sea. It's not very late. But it's already September.

Dora lies on the bed that's still hers. She's hiding from the world. Mom knocks and softly calls her name. Dora! Dorrie! Then nothing more. Dora knows it's the end. Nothing will exist anymore. No more sea. No more clouds. No more long days on the beach. Her fingers beneath the pillow clutch the portrait Luka painted of her. Her sweaty hand smears everything. Everything grows blurry. Like when the mist falls over the sea.

Luka lies on the smooth rock, his legs dangling in the water. He's waiting for Dora. He wishes he had an ice cream now. Strawberry and lemon, of course, not chocolate. He smiles. No way. His right cheek is still warmed by the sun.

. . .

No more barefoot walks. No more ice cream. No more familiar faces. No more round lollipops. She knows the picture is smeared. It's too late. Nothing and no one can be kept safe any longer. If she were to die now, that would be fine by her.

Luka lies on the smooth rock, his legs dangling in the water. He's waiting for Dora. His head hurts a little. He's not in a comfortable position. He doesn't want to pretend. To pretend that he's not afraid.

No more games at the beach. No more cake-filled visits to Aunt Marija, the excellent baker who made chocolate cake just for her, only her—slathered with chocolate cream filling, and glazed in rich chocolate so dark it was almost black. No more harbor. No more ships. Nothing will be recognizable in the picture anymore. Everything. Totally. Ruined.

Luka lies on the smooth rock. As if nothing were happening. Nothing at all. Ever again.

No rock and no cave. No hiding place. No secret home. No dead crabs and beetles. Who could bear it?

Luka lies on the smooth rock. As if he were on another planet. Where nothing is real anymore. A planet that will be forgotten after today. That must be forgotten. As if it had never existed. As long as he waits for Dora, he still lives. He still breathes. Not once does it occur to him to start counting.

. . .

You're still so young, not even seven years old, her mother says.

It's over, the waiting. No more Luka.

As if he were dead. As if she were, too. And the whole world. Dead.
Dead. Deaddeaddeaddeaddeaddeaddeaddeaddeaddeaddead.

Chapter 4

L uka is very excited: It's his first show. It's only at school, of course, but that doesn't matter to him, it's still his first show. Ms. Mesmer, the art teacher, had organized everything. She'd taken the time to go through his paintings, his many paintings, which had almost nothing to do with any instruction he'd ever had in class. She'd looked at them, sorted them and winnowed them, setting some aside, putting some back. She'd removed her glasses from her nose and held the paintings at arm's length, then laid them back down, quietly musing. In the end, she'd singled out twenty watercolors and five oils and set them apart. "Wonderful," was all she said before closing her eyes and sighing deeply. "Wonderful."

On the first Saturday in the last month of school, the time has come at last. The whole middle school is there, the parents, the mayor, relatives, the Party chief, friends. Even the old midwife Anka, with her thick glasses and walking stick, wanted to be there. "You're still my boy," she whispered to him when he came to greet her. A journalist from Split is there, too. Ms. Mesmer has thought of everything. Luka doesn't have to say anything, thank God. He just has to stand there and smile, if he feels like it. Ms. Mesmer introduces him quickly; and then Mr. Mastilica, the principal, praises him copiously, though he's a man of few words, prone to stuttering and slips of the tongue. But nobody laughs, at least not audibly. The principal's face is red and puffy, it's hot, and you can see sweat rings under his arms. He tugs at his necktie several times, as if he weren't getting enough air. Then at last, after he's said "And finally" five times, he's finished. At last people can go look at Luka's paintings. They can walk around the room and look at them as many times as they want. Luka stands on the small stage, which on other occasions is used for dances, recitals and concerts, and looks into the faces of the guests. He can read their expressions: "Wonderful," they say. Ms. Mesmer flits from one group to the next, talking, explaining and answering questions. "Yes, he did it all on his own. He's one of a kind. An unrivaled talent. Those colors. And still so young. Yes, of course they're for sale. The emotion. Yes, I feel the same thing. It's magical. It tells a story. Yes, I can see it, too. So profound. Yes, we're very proud of him. I've always said . . ."

Luka has just turned fifteen, and people already want his pictures hanging in their living rooms. Even if those living rooms are only in Makarska. He has to struggle to keep from closing his eyes. To keep breathing. But soon everything starts to spin, one, two, three, four, five . . .

Ana is by his side, reaching for his hand. She says nothing. She's ten years old. But she seems older when she stands next to him. As if she were about to say with pride, "He's my brother"; but also maybe, "Hold yourself together, open your eyes, don't overdo it." Ana looks after him.

And this warm hand is so charged with memories that Luka does open his eyes, and breathes anew, and though his eyes burn and brim with tears, he doesn't close them again, he's aware that this is his decision, it's the first time in a long time, in an eternity, that he's felt this. He squeezes Ana's hand hard, without asking her any questions. "You're welcome," she says softly, without looking at him. And Luka feels like she's the only person on his private planet. The only one who speaks his silent language.

At the age of twelve, Dora has spent half her life up to now in this foreign land. A land that doesn't feel so foreign anymore. Dora speaks a language that also isn't so foreign anymore, she knows it as well as her native tongue, maybe better. She can say everything, in the right rhythm, with the right inflection, and the right tone. Above all, she's mastered the facial expressions. She's got them down, one hundred percent. *Naturellement.* She's become one of them. *Ah oui, bien sûr.* She can talk about herself in this new language, talk about her family—about her father, Ivan, and the job that brought them here—*mon papa est un architecte*; about her mother, Helena, who was so elated to move here, and who loves Paris—the most beautiful, the most exciting, the most interesting, the most eventful city in the world. She can tell everyone that she comes from Croatia, no, not from Yugoslavia; about her grandparents, who also live in a big city, but in another country, their homeland, a city that's not as big or as pretty as Paris; about their new apartment in the center of Paris, next to a park, the Parc Monceau, where she has a beautiful view of the river from her bedroom, which is much bigger than her old one and has lots of new furniture; about the new neighbors, who are really friendly and nice and have a daughter her age, who she gets along with really well, yes, she would even say she's her best friend, because with Jeanne, that's the girl's name, she always has a fantastic time, and you can totally trust her. Secrets are as safe with Jeanne as the beautiful buildings Dora's dad dreams up, which they can visit, which makes Dora proud to be her father's daughter! These buildings are as safe as Dad's money in the bank—Dad's designs are very sought-after and very expensive—maybe even safer, because banks are often robbed, Jeanne and Dora have read about that in the newspaper. But they feel absolutely safe because Jeanne has a little dog, Papou, who escorts them everywhere and protects them. The three of them have conquered the Parc Monceau, with its curving paths and its statues, which are placed as if at random, small Egyptian pyramids and the Corinthian columns where they play hide-and-seek, and sometimes they just sit beneath the statue of Maupassant or Chopin, talking and whispering, while Papou lies at their feet and sleeps or pretends to sleep, keeping his left eye open. As if he were eavesdropping on their words. Then Dora can gush about her favorite movies and favorite books and favorite music in the new language, which, incidentally, has really won her over, because she's still the same frank, curious, irrepressible girl she always was. In the rose garden, Dora recites verses and long poems to her friend, and sometimes the Spanish concierges who come to the park to take or sneak a break applaud loudly and beg for more. Yes, French has become a very important language to Dora, even though at first she'd been a little afraid of it.

Only about the sea does Dora remain absolutely silent. The sea has only one language. Dora knows that. She feels it. It would be a betrayal to speak of the sea, of the waves, the rock, the seagulls, the diving, the pebble beach, the boat, the lollipop, the seashells, the clouds, in the new language. It would have no meaning. It would just be words, empty words, that anyone could say, that could belong to anyone, and she wouldn't be able to bear it. That is, to renounce something that only she herself has a name for, she and no one else. Or rather, nobody she wants to think about. No one she allows herself to think about. She locks these words in her soul and lets them wander there. And wait. For the prince to come and free them from this tower without doors, where they are at risk of perishing. Where the air is thin.

And one thing she has completely forgotten. In any language.

Chapter 5

Luka doesn't feel like it. He's seventeen years old, he wants to decide for himself. And he doesn't want to leave this place. It's his home. Only here can he paint and live by the sea. Even though everyone says it would be the best thing for his future. Ms. Mesmer can't persuade him, because he's no traitor. Not like some other people he knows. People he used to know, that is. He's not the kind of person who would just go away and leave behind people he likes, who like him.

He doesn't want to believe there's anything he could learn at the art academy at Zagreb that he couldn't learn here in Makarska. The light is here. The colors that give meaning to his life are here. And the sea. Everything is here. The meeting place. How often has his mother told him: "If we ever lose sight of each other, just stay where you are and I will find you. If we both go looking for each other, we'll get lost and never find one another again"? One of them ought to stay where everything happened, one of them has to wait, otherwise each will never find the other again. Where else are they going to meet?!

Besides, he needs to take care of his mother, now that his father is gone, vanished. Zoran just took off on his boat, like a treasure hunter. As if he'd forgotten what the real treasure was, and where it was to be found. And no, he doesn't feel like crying. After all, he's seventeen years old already, he's grown up, he can take care of his family, and obviously, he's not the kind of person who leaves people he loves in the lurch, not like some other people he doesn't know anymore and doesn't need anymore. He's already seventeen, he's grown up.

Luka runs across the woods on the Osejava peninsula as if he were flying, and doesn't encounter anybody along the way. He runs until he's out of breath. If he keeps going, soon he'll be all the way to Tučepi. Could his father be hiding there? If he sees him there, should he turn his head away in contempt and keep going, or should he stop and say hello and ask him how he's doing? Whatever he does, he must not cry. Absolutely not. He's the man of the house now, and men don't do that. Should he beg his father to come home? Nothing feels safe anymore, nothing and nobody. These days, when Picasso's paintings can be stolen right out of the Vatican Palace. One hundred nineteen paintings. No, he will not cry.

Dora's fourteen-year-old face beams radiantly. She sees and hears nothing. Her body glows. She does what she's been taught to do. Above all, she does what it has always lain within her to do, what brings her joy, what fills her every breath. She doesn't have to struggle to find the emotions within her, but she must strive to keep them within herself and not to lose control, and to reveal them only little by little. Because that's how it has to be. Not too much. Not everything at once. The secret of a good actor.

The show is a great success. And not just because the audience is made up of friends and relatives of the young actors. No, it's because of Dora, and the magic that emanates from her, and the emptiness she leaves behind when she exits the stage. Even though it's just a school stage, small and without red velvet curtains. And yet, it was Racine, a genuine, classical, difficult—even if abridged—play by Racine! And she was a fantastic Phaedra, even if the whole play and all the roles had to be adapted for the kids on the stage and in the audience. An achievement worthy of the Comédie-Française! Dora can't stop replaying the show in her mind, she lives and dies a thousand more times before she rejoins the others. She doesn't want to come out of character, she doesn't want to stop being a tragic heroine, or to renounce the false identity that doesn't feel false to her at all. This is her life. As it's always been. She closes her eyes and sees herself in a mirror, a little girl who can control the muscles of her face, who can master her expression, who knows what she's doing at every moment. This is not a game, this is who she is. She is everything at once, combined. The whole world, whether the world notices her or not.

If the world around her goes in one direction and she goes in another, it doesn't matter. Good wishes, hugs, kisses, joyful laughter. That's her, and it isn't her. Jeanne is near her. That much she can recognize. Jeanne tugs at her arm; she seems to want either to shake her or to take her away from there. Dora's not sure which, but it's all the same to her. There's nothing at all she wants right now. If only it could stay this way. If only everything could stay the way it is now. Phaedra forever. Because everything is finally clear. As clear as the sky over Paris can be, on rare occasions. She feels serene in her excitement; for once she isn't impelled by the drive to do more. At last she can stand still. She's found her calling.

"Do you see, he's there, looking at you, he can't help himself, he can't take his eyes off of you," Jeanne whispers, and Dora hears her without quite understanding. But she does see a large form, a boy; a boy who is shyly but resolutely standing at the stage door, and following her with his eyes. Dora thinks she knows him. He's two classes above her, she's often seen him in the hallway at school, blue eyes, long blond hair, he must be an athlete, basketball, yes, that's right, she saw him play in a game once. He was good. Maybe not the standout player of the night, but very good. Quick. Gérard. His name was Gérard. Right. Every time he passes her in the hallway, he gives her a slight, almost imperceptible nod. She doesn't know what she's supposed to make of it. Especially not today. It's not like he's Hippolytus. But the way he's standing there, looking at her so shyly, makes her throat catch. She suddenly has the feeling, a feeling that passes over her like a cloud, that she's somewhere else, that she is someone else. She feels short of breath: If she were somebody else, she would surely faint at this moment.

"I think he's coming over!" Jeanne whispers in excitement, and squeezes Dora's hand so hard that it hurts. The pressure frees Dora from the oppressive feeling that weighs down her chest, her head, her whole body. It brings her back to herself; and then this Gérard is just a guy named Gérard again, and everything is fine, and she can breathe freely again and be a wonderful Phaedra.

And it's true that Gérard is no Hippolytus, but that probably isn't a bad thing—Hippolytus doesn't care for Phaedra anyway!—but the smile that lights up his whole face and the gleam in his eyes makes her aware of her breathing. Maybe there will be another performance today, one that nobody had told her about. Briefly, she feels something like panic, but the feeling evaporates almost immediately, because she can be anyone, play any role, and she's good at improvising. Nothing can go wrong.

Chapter 6

"Please, open up!" Ana's voice is muffled, but determined and persistent, all the more so because of its gentleness. You might think you could hide from her, or escape her, but it's an illusion. Even through the closed door, his sister's voice is full of strength. Even in this situation.

Luka lies on the bed in his parents' house and cries. Quietly. He's not sad. He's enraged. He lies on his back, stares at the ceiling and imagines that it's the sky and he's lying on the beach, and the dark spots are clouds . . . And immediately he knows that this is a gigantic mistake. Some taboos are taboos for good reason. And should never, ever be broken.

Like, for instance, looking at the clouds. Or even thinking about looking at them.

At this moment, his anger begins to mingle with grief. Ana's words fall like raindrops. Swift raindrops, without number.

"Please let me in, please!"

She may be saying "please," but she doesn't mean it. It's an order. It doesn't occur to Ana that anyone would contradict her. She's sweet and kind and genuine. But she's also strong. Though she's only thirteen years old.

Like Dad, Luka thinks. Strong like Dad. He envies her for it. He wishes he were like Dad. That confidence and security. Even though Dad's not around anymore.

Dad left them the year before, just moved out. Just like that, moved to a totally different city. He took his boat and disappeared. Even though Luka has his address, and can visit him or call him anytime he wants, it still feels to him like Dad has disappeared. Gone missing. He's no longer where he's supposed to be. With him. With Ana. With their mother. He ran away. Just like that. And even though his departure was preceded by countless warning signs over the years, when it finally happened, it happened suddenly. Nobody had really believed it was possible. Nobody. Except for Ana. And Mother. And their relatives. And the neighbors. And their friends. And everyone who knew him. It was only his son who was surprised. It was as if Luka's eyes had been full of clouds. Or paint. For years, Luka had watched the happiness drain slowly from his father's face. His laughter. His joy in life. His father had shrouded himself in silence, had hidden from the world behind empty eyes. He had withdrawn from Luka, his son. His buddy. He was only ever to be found on his boat. Until the day when he was totally gone. And nobody said anything about it. As if it were the most normal thing in the world. No questions, nothing. Luka was the only one who walked around like a crazy person, searching for his father. "Grow up," Ana, his little sister, said. Their mother just looked the other way and kept silent. Luka had the feeling she didn't even blame his father. As if they'd come to an agreement. But Luka hadn't agreed to anything! He'd been betrayed and abandoned, and there was nothing he could do about it. There was no longer any point to walking around looking for his father, as he'd started doing a year ago, when it happened; it would solve nothing. If he'd run into his father back then, maybe everything might have turned out differently. But now! What a pointless exercise! So ridiculous. So pathetic.

Other people have made choices for him. Again. "Grow up," Ana, his little sister, told him.

"No, I don't want to."

"You don't love me."

Gérard turns away from Dora and hangs his head. Dora isn't sure if he's really hurt or offended or sad, or if the whole thing is some kind of game, to cajole her. They've been going out for a year now. It's been a nice year. Dora likes the way Gérard treats her. He's so good to her, and her heart beats faster when he holds her hand. In January they went together to the opening of the Centre Georges Pompidou, and later in the year, they stood among the crowds at the train station when the Orient Express made its last Paris-Istanbul trip, and in April, when Jacques Prévert died, she recited his poems to Gérard for hours and they cried together, she'd cried more than he had, but that doesn't mean anything. She trusts him. And still. There's something she doesn't understand, something that makes her doubt, makes her hold back. She longs for his kisses, his embraces. He strokes her hair so tenderly. He always tells her he loves her hair. How it shines. She likes the way he says her name. The way he whispers it in her ear. The way his lips lightly brush her and make her tremble.

But she doesn't love him. She's sure of it. She just can't tell him that. Because she does like him. She feels comfortable with him. She doesn't want to break up with him. Not remotely. She just doesn't want to sleep with him.

She's only fifteen years old. That's too early.

"I can't yet." It's a white lie. Because she will never want to sleep with Gérard. She knows this, without knowing why. She knows he won't be her first lover. It's not a feeling, it's a conviction that she owns fully, the same way that she owns the stage when she stands on it and speaks her lines, or when she keeps silent, or when she simply watches her fellow actors.

"Why not?"

She can't say anything. Above all, she can't tell him the truth.

"What are you waiting for? What's missing?"

The sea, she wants to say. The clouds. The rock . . . She begins to shiver. The feeling that there was once something there. Someone. Still is. Maybe.

Luka lies on his bed and stares at the ceiling. It's been such a long time, so many years. Half his life. The mute half. The dead half. The half that he tried to bring to life by painting. An overdose of time. An abundance of paint. And silence.

Dora ran away from Gérard, she could find no other way out, because the right words wouldn't come to her. She fled. And now she sits in the big, cozy armchair in her bedroom, in the empty apartment. Her father's away on a trip. Her mother's at the office. Probably. Dora is alone in this giant apartment that is so far from the most important things. From herself and her life. From a life away from the stage, in which she has to generate her own words. Years filled with silence and blindness. She doesn't move. She doesn't want to search. She has the feeling, one she's often felt during these years, that it would be dangerous to search. To find. To see. How has it come to this? "It's just your age, pure and simple," her mother would say.

Kid stuff. If only Luka could believe it. Could forget everything. Maybe now's the right time to get out of here. Now that everyone is gone. Father vanished. Mother dead.

The telephone rings. Dora remains seated, motionless. She needs to think. She marvels at the thought that some things are even more important to her than acting. Because she's not thinking about her next role in the new play, which will go up at the end of the school year. Sartre. She likes Camus better, finds his language gentler. But Dora's not thinking about that now. No. She's trying to remember. There was something. The harbor. A small town. With only a few streets broad enough for cars. No stoplights. There were boats there. Lots of little boats. And it hardly ever rained. There was delicious chocolate ice cream. And cake. And jolly round lollipops. And the people were really nice. It was hot in summer there. Very hot. And she had a blue swimsuit, from Italy. Her father had given it to her. With tiny glittering stones on it that flickered in the water like the scales on a mermaid's tail. In the sea, not in ordinary water. The rough grains made the difference. They felt so good on her body, and when they dried, they left a funny white pattern on her skin. Her skin would contract and create a pleasing tautness, a feeling of happiness. The phone rings again and Dora remains seated. The name won't come to her. How is it that she can't remember the name?!

.   .   .

Luka lies on his bed and looks at the ceiling.

He'd come home from school an hour earlier than usual. Math, his last class, had been canceled, which was good, because he hadn't done his homework. "Mom," he'd called out, "I'm home." Nothing. But that wasn't unusual, his mother hadn't left her bed for months. Ever since Dad left, she'd been sick. Without a diagnosis. Without medication. Without hope. So maybe Luka wasn't the only one who'd felt betrayed and abandoned, after all. After a while, he'd quit worrying about her. Because he felt so stupid whenever he tried to cheer her up. Like a clown. Everything was pointless. He went to the kitchen and got an apple. Took a bite. Greedily. He stared out the window. It was a hot spring day. He wanted to go to the beach and paint a little before water polo practice. Suddenly, the silence began to bother him. Something about it drove him to go to his mother's room. She lay there, her head turned to the door, as if she'd been waiting for him. Her eyes were open. "Mom?" Eyes open and motionless. "Mom!" Of course, he understood everything at once. Of course, he didn't want to understand. He went to her.

"Mom." Very softly. He touched her outstretched arm. It was cool. "Mom." He laid his hand on her forehead. Cool. Dry. "Mom." He bent down low and looked into her face. Her lips were slightly parted. As if she were smiling. Luka couldn't remember the last time he had seen his mother smile. Let alone laugh. "Mom." It came as no surprise that she was silent and didn't answer. Luka sat next to her on the bed. "Mom." His finger traced her face. It was relaxed. Peaceful. Almost contented. The word *serene* came to him. Luka laid his head on her breast and closed his eyes. "Mom." He heard nothing. No heartbeat. His head didn't move. Not one millimeter. Not one nano-

meter. Her breast was like stone. But soft. Excruciatingly soft. "Mom."
He stroked her head. Her cheeks. Her throat. Her narrow shoulders.
Her arms. And then, again, her head. Her hair. Her cheeks. Her
throat. Her narrow shoulders. Her arms. And then, again, her head . . .
"Mom."

It was at that moment that Ana arrived. "Mom!" she screamed.
Cried. "Mom, no, please, no, no, Mom, no, please, Mom . . ."

Luka stood up and hugged Ana. Not for very long. He didn't wait
for her to calm down. No. Ana kept on crying. Wailing. Loudly and
without cease.

Without a word, Luka went to his room, and shut himself
in. Betrayed and abandoned. And stared at the ceiling. For hours
on end.

Dora closes her eyes, sensing salt on her skin, in her mouth. Such a
familiar taste. A little bitter. The phone rings again. That name! A
person should be able to summon up a name! Makarska, yes, that one,
of course, that's no secret. But the other one.

Maybe he actually should go to the art academy and do something
about his future. Something completely new. Yes, that wouldn't be
bad at all. The idea pleases him. This time, for a change, he will be the
one to go away, to leave everyone else behind. There's no sense in staying here and waiting, holding down the fort. For whom? Everyone's
gone.

"Luka, open the door! We've got to talk, we've got to call the doctor, and arrange the funeral. We have decisions to make. Please!"

Yes, Ana's right. He's got to make decisions. To grow up.

. . .

The telephone rings again. Dora remains seated, motionless. She has to think things over. She has to embark on this journey full of memories, even if she has no visa for it. Emotions surge and vanish before she can grasp them. But she understands that this is important. If she wants to move forward, she needs to do this now. To let herself go. To forget herself in order to remember. The sea under the bright sky. She must start there. It's not in the south of France, no. Not where she and her parents went. And not in Brittany either, no, not at all. There must be another sea. Fear will be her guide. Her signpost. To the rock. She sobs loudly, but remembers nothing. What is she afraid of?

He opens the door, and in a moment of clarity—and confusion—he sees a scrawny, dark-haired little girl before him, who smiles up at him with big, black eyes, holds her hand out to him, and takes him with her . . .

"Finally!"

Ana is only thirteen, but she's as wise as Toma, the old fisherman who sits by his boat in the harbor, unchanging, fussing with his nets or his pipe. Whose dark face, etched with sun, wind and salt, radiates warmth. Old Uncle Toma always has time on his hands. He doesn't talk much. But you can sit with him and tell stories if you like. Or sit with him and keep silent. Either way, you feel better afterward. A lot better. That's for sure. You regain your confidence, feel ready to take the next step. You're no longer afraid, you feel optimistic about what's to come. Ready to let yourself be surprised by life again.

Luka hugs his little sister and holds her tight. She needs him.

Obviously. Maybe he can help her. That would be wonderful. To be able to help someone. To be there for another person. To keep somebody in his life.

At six, are you too young?

"I'm sorry, I'm so sorry . . ." Luka cries in Ana's hair. It's thick and honey-blond and long, and he could bury himself in it. But he doesn't. He's hidden himself away long enough. He's done with hiding. Now he's going to make decisions, and do what it takes to keep things from getting even harder. Ana is quiet in his arms. Luka doesn't know what she's feeling, whether it's relief or anger, whether she believes him or not. "I'll take care of everything, don't worry, I'll take care of it," he tells her. Ana doesn't move, she breathes softly and trembles, and then she's quiet again. "I'm sorry, I left you on your own too long, I'm sorry, I'll make things right again, I promise you, everything will be all right . . ." He might as well be talking to himself, quieting his own fears.

"I want Dad to come home." Ana's voice is as clear as the sea in winter.

It's that easy.

The question is: For what? Too young for what?

It's nighttime. Luka isn't sleeping. His sister lies next to him on the bed. She breathes calmly and regularly, smiling a little in her sleep. Luka is not surprised. Yes, her mother died today, but she's smiling because her father is coming home. She's still a little girl, after all.

Thirteen years old. How big is the difference between thirteen and fifteen? At fifteen, are you still a kid? Sometimes it seems to him that the last time he was a kid was when he was three. But not everyone is like him. Fifteen can mean anything.

Too young for life. For the rest of your life, you could say. If, at the age of six, everything has been determined, what remains for the future? The question rages in Dora's head like a fever.

Luka gets up and goes to the wardrobe, opens it softly. He doesn't want to wake Ana. Way down, in the deepest, most forgotten corner, lies a wooden box that he painted many years before with nautical motifs, gluing seashells onto it for decoration. He rests his hand on it. Nothing happens. His hand doesn't get bitten, doesn't get burned. Nonetheless, he removes the box with caution. He doesn't remember exactly what's inside.

The moon is round and full and shines brightly into the room. He needs no other light. He sets the box on the carpet in front of his crossed legs. It's heavier than he expected. He looks at it and puts both his hands on it. His fingers move as if of their own volition, and there he sits, in the middle of the night, stroking a small wooden box. He's eighteen, but tonight he feels like an eight-year-old. Because it was when he was nine that . . .

To Dora, it feels like she's putting together a puzzle. As if she had all the important pieces, but no box-cover picture to guide her. It seems hopeless. Maybe even ridiculous, delusional kid stuff. Maybe she's just growing up. "It's your age, pure and simple," her mother would say. Yes, maybe so. If only she didn't have this feeling. If only there weren't a box, someplace in this apartment, filled with her things from another life. From another life that was somehow hers, too. The telephone rings. Damn it! Dora gets up and leaves the room. The apartment. She slams the door behind her, as if it were a verdict.

On the morning after the funeral Luka visits his art teacher at her home. Ms. Mesmer lives in an old stone house on the edge of the city, where the coastal road heads off to Dubrovnik. She lives alone. Her husband died ten years ago. He was a painter. His paintings hang all over the house. No photographs; at least, none in the hall or in the living room. Luka and Ms. Mesmer sit on the terrace. She brings out iced tea, and Luka feels very grown up.

They drink and keep silent. It's a comfortable silence. They look out at the sea. There's a pleasant view from the terrace, you can see the peninsulas of Saint Petar and Osejava. It's 9:45, the ferry to Sumartin is leaving the harbor. Luka is in no hurry. He feels the tension slide out of him. He settles comfortably in the soft, cushioned wicker chair.

"I saw your father. He's back, that's good news." Ms. Mesmer doesn't look at him. She busies herself with her glass.

"Yes, it's good."

"I've heard he's going to take over the small hotel in Donja Luka."

"Yes, supposedly."

"That's good."

"Yes, it's good."

And again they fall silent.

"You have a nice house."

"Yes, it's nice, isn't it?"

They drink and keep silent. Luka feels as if time were standing still. As if there were no such thing as time. He closes his eyes and thinks of nothing. He's a real master when the situation calls for thinking of nothing.

"So, you've changed your mind?" She lowers her head a little, and looks at him over the rim of her glasses. He doesn't respond.

"That's good, I'm very happy." She takes a sip of iced tea. "You have the greatest talent of anyone I've ever taught, or known personally. I'm so pleased."

She puts down her glass. It catches the sunbeams, glinting with bright colors.

"It's the only thing I've ever wanted to do. My whole life. I've wanted to paint. Nothing but to paint. That glass there that caught the light. The sea at all times, in all weather."

"Good."

"The sea and the light. I want to paint what's inside me."

She keeps still for a few moments. She looks at him intently. Not as if she were seeing him for the first time. No. But as if she had always already known this about him.

"That can be painful."

It's the only thing she says.

When they've sat in silence more than long enough, she gets up, takes a stamped envelope from the top drawer of the dresser in the living room and gives it to him. Luka grasps the thin letter, looking at his teacher as he takes it. Embarrassed and excited at the same time.

"This letter has been waiting for you for too long. It will make your path a little easier. But only externally."

They are at the door.

"See you tomorrow at school, then," she says, and lays her hand on his cheek. Lovingly. Consolingly. Full of faith in him.

And Luka thinks of his mother. Who is dead. Forever and ever. Vanished into the warm earth.

Before the first tears can come to his eyes, he turns swiftly and rushes to the street. He's practically running. But he won't get hit by a car. No, that's not his fate. Besides, there aren't enough cars yet in Makarska in 1977.

Chapter 7

She's made it. She belongs. To the favored few. The deed is done. Dora can't help grinning. It's obvious, even though she knows that it's everything but obvious. She climbs the stairway, following the others, who are also on their way to paradise. She knows that everything will go according to her plan, which is basically preordained; there's never been a real alternative for her. This is the only way that all of the lives that clamor within her for expression can be liberated. And even though Sartre died in April, his plays remain, and she'll be able to act in all of them. Someday.

And while she's pursuing her future, she's accosted by a vision; a mosaic of tiny fragments of another life buried deep within her, bringing her feelings of certainty, security and happiness. She doesn't want to examine this vision too closely, maybe for fear of missing it, were it to go away. The fragments are as sharp as the dry rims of seashells, as soft as melting ice in summer, as warm as fresh-baked bread, and as well defined as clouds in spring, shaped by strong gusts of northern wind. And all of these shards are embedded in the glittering blue of the sea. They aren't memories, they are the life Dora has forgotten, the life that stands before her. Everything is bound together in mysterious ways. Distinct and contrasting, but linked all the same.

Because Dora is there, at her first acting class at the French National Academy of Dramatic Arts, in Paris. Everything will come together. This is her passionate conviction.

"I love you." Klara's words caress his ear. Luka lays down his paintbrush and turns to her. She doesn't put her arms around him. She keeps the proscribed distance from his body. The rule is, she mustn't touch him when he's working. But she always finds new ways to disturb his concentration, to call attention to herself. He likes it and he doesn't like it, because he's fond of her but he doesn't want to be distracted. Even when he's not pressed for time. Though he's never behind on a deadline. His work is ready before the instructors even have made their assignments. He lives to paint. Brushstrokes are his oxygen. Does Klara understand this?

Klara is wonderful. Like him, she comes from Makarska, but she moved to Zagreb so long ago that Luka doesn't know her from before. Besides, she's three years older than he is. Klara teaches dance. They met two years ago in the hospital, when Luka was visiting a friend who'd broken both arms in a car accident. Klara was lying in the next room, woozy from strong painkillers. A badly broken leg. It was the number-one topic of discussion among the nurses and the patients, because Klara had acquired some local renown for her dancing, and the break put an unfortunate end to her promising career. Luka had decided to visit her, even brought her flowers to cheer her up and console her. He realized that the two of them had a lot in common. Their birthplace, for example. That's how it all began. And Klara hadn't given up after the accident. After she'd cried herself out, she dried her wide-set eyes and smiled. As if to say, There are worse fates. Which was true of course. And yet. Luka marveled at her resilience. Klara says it was love at first sight. She'd seen Luka in her drugged half-sleep, thought she was dreaming at first, and when he turned out to be a real person, she knew at once: He's the one. "It was as clear to me as my love for dance," she liked to say.

As for himself, Luka can't say it was love at first sight. For him, that had happened long before and somewhere else. That's right. It was such a long time ago that he hardly ever thinks about it anymore. About that first look. That's over and done with. But it was the first all the same. Everyone knows that you can fall in love at first sight only once. He's never told Klara about it. Of course not. Luka doesn't know too much about women, he lacks experience. Even though he's already twenty-one years old. Or maybe because of that, it's hard to say. But he knows that no woman would like to hear that. Especially a woman in love. He's painted a portrait of Klara all the same. The picture hangs in the dancing school where she teaches. They don't live together. Not yet, Klara says; and Luka makes no comment. He really can't imagine living with her. He likes Klara, and he doesn't want anything to change. Everything's just fine the way it is. Sometimes he thinks he can't stand intimacy. But then Ana comes over, and Luka can't get enough of her. He's noticed that Klara watches him intently during Ana's visits, and he imagines she makes false assumptions, but it doesn't bother him. Probably because Ana and Klara get along so well.

Ana likes Klara. Klara takes a warm interest in her, mothers her, even, and Ana doesn't object. It makes Luka think that his little sister still misses her mother. Even though she's got Dad at home now, who's almost become his old self again. Ana and Zoran live together like two friends, in the little house by the sea near the hotel that Zoran has been running for three years. Ana wants to be a teacher, and to stay in Makarska. She's head over heels in love, Toni is his name, they're in the same year at school. He plays water polo like Luka did, back in the day, before he moved to Zagreb and turned his full attention to painting. Toni is tall, strong and good-looking, and he's in love with Ana. Sometimes Luka thinks he's missing some essential element, that something has passed him by, or been stolen from him. The lightness of youth. Seeing his sister, he tells himself: Life can be so easy.

But the truth is that his own life isn't much more complicated than hers. He does what he wants to do, he has a girlfriend he likes who loves him, and he's already sold some of his paintings—he's not making enough money to live on, but things are gradually coming together. No obvious barriers, no obstacles in his path.

And yet. There's something that shouldn't be there, even if he has no doubt that it's part of who he is.

"I love you."

Dora believes André, believes that he loves her. And she likes him, too. Even if she's never told him she loves him. It doesn't come easily to her. Whenever the words want to come out, they get stuck somewhere between her throat and her tongue before she's summoned the breath to pronounce them, as if they'd taken fright. As if they were afraid of the light.

"I love you."

Dora hugs him. In place of tender words.

André is wonderful. They'd met only a few months before, six months, to be exact, but already Dora feels at ease with him, feels at home. André is four years older, he's almost finished his studies—he's in finance—and he works in his father's bank. Because he's so smart and hardworking. And because he knows everything about money, unlike Dora. André likes to laugh lovingly at her naïveté about money. "When you get rich and famous, please leave your financial affairs to me."

"Gladly," she responds. It's all the same to Dora. She doesn't think about it. She's got other things on her mind.

"Let's go out to eat. A new restaurant has opened around the corner. The food is supposed to be exceptional."

"And expensive."

"Don't worry about that, that's my affair. I want to spoil my starlet." He takes her hand and prepares to go.

"You're a snob," Dora says, mildly amused, making no move to take a single step.

"As long as you want to have me on your arm . . ."

"But I'm really not hungry at all. And I've got to learn my lines. It's the first day, and we've already got homework!" She continues to stand, unmoving, looking around.

"But you've got to eat! I'll help with your lines afterward."

"That would be something new!"

She laughs. All he has ever helped her do is get into bed.

He turns her toward him and wraps his arms around her. He rests his chin on her head: André is tall.

"It's not my fault that you're so sweet that I can't keep my hands off you, that every single minute I want your soft mouth, your firm breasts, your . . ."

"Stop, stop, stop! You see, that's exactly what I mean!"

She's only pretending to be angry, she lets him kiss her, lets his hands stroke her body. Even in the middle of the street. She feels desire rise in her, she closes her eyes, she's feeling good, she hears him softly moan in her ear . . .

"I've got to go now . . ." But she says it with less conviction.

"You're horrible, such behavior is forbidden . . ." His mouth is still on her ear.

"But I've got to. It's not like I don't want to."

"Then, let's go to my place, in my superfast car, we'll be there in a flash, think of the bed, big and warm and . . ."

"You're crazy."

"Then, let's go to your place."

"I'll go to my apartment, and you go back to your bank, and we can meet tonight instead, and I promise you even a little bonus, if you'll just leave now, and let me learn my lines . . ."

He takes his arms off her so lightning-fast that she almost falls over. Her legs are unsteady without the support of his hands. A momentary sensation of regret, of missing him, of undesired rejection, hits her in the gut like a balled-up fist.

But she lets him go. She's fine with a good-bye that isn't final. Did she hear someone laughing? That's her new role, to make herself a laughingstock, pure and simple, her mother would say. A person doesn't always have to explain herself, Dora thinks, and hurries home.

"I love you," Klara whispers.

Luka stands up, and pauses, facing her. She's still not touching him. She probably thinks she's abiding by their rule. They look at each other. Then Luka smiles and lays his arms on her shoulder.

"What smells so good?"

She takes his hand and leads him into the kitchen. A galley kitchen. It's small and impractical and inadequately equipped for a cook as skilled as Klara. But she always manages to whip up something delicious for the two of them. He loves it when she cooks for him. There's something intimate and soothing about it. Especially when she bakes something. Whether it's a cake or vegetables au gratin, it's the same to him. The oven radiates a warmth that has nothing to do with physical heat. The warmth of home. Of safety. Of summer on the beach. Of the midday sun.

"Prepare to be surprised."

They eat at the tastefully laid table, which is actually an uneven board set on three shaky legs.

Luka gets full quickly. He doesn't eat a lot. He likes to eat, but he doesn't eat much. He leans back in his chair, not too far back, because then it might collapse. Luka smiles at Klara contentedly. She gives him her hand. He takes it without hesitation.

"And now I want to sleep with you."

When Dora comes home, her mother and father are sitting quietly in the living room in their armchairs, staring at the door. And neither of them says "I love you." It's very unusual for her father, who earns his living designing blueprints and construction plans for exclusive apartments and houses, to be home before seven P.M. And normally, her mother would be out lunching with some promising young author whose book she absolutely must acquire for her tiny publishing company.

"Who died?"

Dora remains standing at the door. Her father looks at her mother, who obviously does not want to return his glance. But she smiles awkwardly at her daughter, looking like a child who knows she's done something naughty but hopes nobody will notice or scold her.

"We're getting divorced. Pure and simple."

And Luka goes to bed with Klara. He makes love to her passionately and sensually, while images form in his head. Kissing her mouth, he longs for a paintbrush. He strokes her smooth body as if it were a canvas he was painting with his fingers.

"Your mother has fallen in love."

Her father's voice is sarcastic and hurt, skeptical and aggrieved. He repeatedly takes off his glasses, polishes them, puts them back on, takes them off, polishes them, puts them back on. He does it so many times that Dora starts to get dizzy. She turns her gaze from him and looks at her mother, who's propped upright in the chair, staring straight ahead, as if she were engrossed in a fascinating painting.

"We're getting divorced. Pure and simple."

"You wish!"

"I don't want to spend one more day with you. Let alone a night."

"Oh, right. So you say."

"It's over, Ivan."

"I can't accept that."

"There's nothing for you to accept. It's just the way it is."

"Who says?"

"I say."

"Since when do you decide such things all by yourself?"

"Since I stopped loving you."

Dora leaves the room. It's like a bad movie come to life, she thinks. They'll work things out. She shuts the door of her bedroom behind her and stops listening. An unnatural silence envelops her. As if she were the last living creature after the end of the world. She lies down on her bed and puts on some music. Jazz. A saxophone and a piano. That's all she needs. Her mother says that, at eighteen, she's still too young for jazz, it's just wrong. Purely and simply wrong. But that's Dora all over, she's always got to be different, and sometimes it's purely and simply impossible for a mother to get along with a daughter like this. The music's soft, deep tones surge in Dora's ears like waves at dusk. Love, jealousy and death. She feels a tightness in her chest.

"Ana's coming to visit tomorrow." Luka's voice betrays mild excitement. Klara looks at him and smiles vacantly but contentedly, as if she were still caught up in the moment that has just passed.

"And? How do you like my new apartment?"

"I can't believe you already have your own apartment, Mom! It's only been one day!"

"I've been renting it for months. I purely and simply had to get everything ready—for the separation, I mean."

"I don't want to hear about it!"

Nevertheless, Dora looks around her mother's new apartment. It's small, minuscule compared to the apartment in which they had been a family until the day before yesterday. But it's inviting and comfortable and filled with light, and Dora can hardly bring herself to leave it.

"I want to have my own apartment, too."

Her mother takes her hand and leads her to the small living room. They sit beside each other on the sofa.

"Are you furious with me?" Softly, very softly, she asks the question, as if she fears the answer.

Dora turns to her mother and looks into her moist eyes. She smiles. She lays her head on her mother's shoulder, as if she were a very sleepy little girl who doesn't want to go to bed.

"I really do love him."

Dora nods, full of understanding, but her mother keeps talking.

"And he loves me."

Dora believes her. Her mother is beautiful, and funny, and caring. And she has a way of looking at you that makes you grateful for every breath you take.

"He really loves me."

The doorbell rings.

"Take it easy, you're hugging me too hard!"

But Luka laughs and holds Ana really tight, so she knows not to take him seriously. She hangs on his neck, and kisses him all over. Her boyfriend, Toni, stands behind her, smiling awkwardly. Zoran stands behind Toni, he looks happy. Klara stands by the window, watching them all closely, as if she doesn't belong. And she doesn't. It's an unexpected revelation for Luka, something he can't bring himself to acknowledge at this moment, it's too brutal.

So he gives Toni his hand and claps him on his strong water polo player's shoulder. Seeing Toni sparks memories. Practices at the Seagull sports club, the smell of chlorine. And then he's standing across from his father, and he feels like sobbing. Every time he sees this man, his love for him overpowers him like something new, unexpected, unique, even. Maybe it has something to do with the gentle, lingering scent of sea and sun and fresh air, of boats and fish and warm breezes, that his father carries with him. Fleeting visions fill Luka's head, and he can neither think them away nor paint them. An insatiable longing gnaws at him. Father and son embrace. They don't say a word. Their glances meet, and that's enough. That's how it's always been.

"Let's go eat. Klara has booked a table at the best restaurant in Zagreb."

"I get it, that means the old man will be paying." Zoran laughs in satisfaction. Nothing pleases him more than spending money on his children.

"Of course! Why else have a hotel manager for a father?" Klara says, and Luka feels uneasy.

But everybody laughs. Ana hugs Toni and gives him a quick kiss. At the age of sixteen, she still finds it awkward to show affection for another man in front of her father and brother. Luka rests his arm on Zoran's shoulder. At the door, he turns around, almost as an afterthought.

"Klara, are you coming?"

"Dora, this is Marc. Marc, this is my daughter, Dora."

Marc is young, handsome, tall and dark-haired, with black eyes. Young. He smiles at Dora with his big, soft mouth. Young. He lays a muscular arm on Helena's shoulders. Very young.

The silence lasts too long. Dora is aware of that. But she can't move her lips. She can't stop staring. She can't believe it. Then again, who wouldn't fall in love with such a man? Standing beside her, they make a beautiful couple. Despite the age difference. And they are happy. Beaming. Delighted with themselves. Besotted. Even if neither of them says "I love you." At least, not out loud, and not in front of her.

"We want to invite you to dinner, we want to celebrate with you."

Dora hardly recognizes her mother. She looks at her with a mixture of shyness, suspicion, excitement and pride. And thinks of her father, who is still handsome, but who's got a good twenty years on Marc. She feels she ought to show solidarity with her father, to turn down the invitation, give this new man the cold shoulder, criticize her mother. The words *must, should, want,* and *can* stage a battle scene in her head like surreal images in a cartoon: irons flying into faces, heads bashed by frying pans, brooms getting swallowed up.

"What is there to celebrate?" Dora's voice shakes a little, as if she were tired of all this *Tom and Jerry* action.

Helena and Marc look at each other conspiratorially but with total openness. The atmosphere around them seems to glow. Dora is only eighteen, and all this is decidedly too much for her. She thinks of André. Do the two of them glow like this when they're together? She takes a deep breath. She feels like she's been drawn into an unusually challenging dramatic exercise.

"Us."

That's how simple life can be. Simpler than any play. Simpler than anything she's ever seen onstage. Dora lowers her eyes. She's afraid she's going to cry. Her mother gives her time. She knows Dora better than anyone. She knows the exuberant little girl who could never get enough of anything. And even though Dora's almost grown up, things like that don't change, she's probably counting on that. Helena looks at Marc and gives him a reassuring smile. Dora sees it, that is, she senses it without actually seeing it.

"But I have plans with André. We were also going to go to a fancy restaurant."

Dora still doesn't look at them. She's well versed in methods of deception. It's as if she carries a magician's bag of tricks with her at all times that she can plunder at will, whenever she needs to.

"Is it for a special occasion?"

It's Marc who asks. He has a mellow, deep voice that makes Dora think of warm, molten caramel. The kind that sticks to your teeth. If his eyes were green . . .

"Us," Dora answers pertly, raising her eyes. Marc's eyes seem to laugh at her. They're black. That's good. She couldn't take it if they were green. She sees a question mark in Helena's eyes, which are also black, nearly as dark as Dora's.

"Then, can the two of us couples celebrate together?"

"Maybe."

"Come on, sweetie! Do us the pleasure!"

"We'll see . . ."

"Call André right now, and tell him that, pure and simple, we'll all meet at the restaurant Chez Moi, it's the crème de la crème."

"It's pretty new."

Dora looks at the two of them. She doesn't know what to do.

"Do we want to invite Dad, too?"

"This tastes wonderful!"

All mouths are full, and all heads nod in enthusiastic agreement.

Luka sits between Klara and Ana. From time to time, he feels Klara's hand on his knee. But it's a well-behaved hand, it keeps its place, and doesn't stray.

"When are you two getting married?"

Ana lobs the question into the room casually, as if by accident and yet perfectly planned. It floats above their table in the fragrant dining room, above the tomato soup that tastes of the sun, and the bouillabaisse that exhales a rich, garlicky aroma. Uncomfortable noises follow; a cleared throat, a cough, then nothing.

Luka is overcome by a feeling he can't define. It leaves him momentarily deaf and dumb. His eyes dart around like canaries in a cage that's too small for them. Breathe, he's got to breathe, and if he keeps his eyes open, and doesn't count, and keeps breathing . . .

"Just kidding, big brother! Got you!"

Ana laughs loudly at her joke, but nobody joins in. Everyone feels a little embarrassed, almost ashamed.

"You're so childish." Toni doesn't quite look at Ana, he just shakes his head. And Luka looks around the restaurant, which, though it's new and the food is great, somehow reminds him of the old socialist restaurants, where the waiters take no joy in their work and more or less openly hate the guests. Tito's death hasn't changed anything. Or not yet. And maybe it's better that way. Kokoschka's death hadn't changed anything either. And even if Luka didn't like all his paintings, he recognized the greatness, and admired it.

"What, don't you guys have a sense of humor?"

"Some jokes aren't funny." Zoran gives his daughter a serious look.

"Klara, say something, you knew I was kidding, right?"

Klara says nothing. She's leaning forward, her head droops, hovering above the bouillabaisse in her soup bowl, though her back is as straight as a proper dancer's should be. Luka doesn't like the situation at all. This should not have happened. He feels like he's shrinking into himself, melting into the air. Like he's standing next to himself, observing himself as if he were a stranger.

"I'm pregnant."

Luka takes a long walk. A walk that cannot be long enough. He has the uncomfortable feeling of being unable to make any decision at all, much less the right one. Because Luka is gone now. As good as dead.

Chapter 8

It's Dora's evening. It's her flowers that fill the room almost to bursting. It's her friends, raising their glasses to toast her. This could be heaven. Or maybe something better. And tomorrow morning she begins her rehearsals as a professional actress. Her first professional engagement. Cordelia. She still thinks she must be dreaming. Cordelia, her first role. She's so happy she could start crying all over again. The world revolves around her, as she's always imagined. The year is 1984.

André is beside her. For four years now, André has always been by her side, and today his face is flushed with excitement. Again and again he kisses her, and she smiles without fully registering his presence, because tonight is her night, today was her graduation performance, and she'd pulled it off, created something new out of nothing. When the curtain fell, everyone in the audience sat in speechless amazement for a few moments, staring straight ahead, until the first member of the examination committee stood up and began to applaud. Cries of "Brava!" rang out. And she let herself be congratulated and embraced. People tried to speak to her, but she wasn't really present; she was still Antigone, her whole body overcome with trembling. Then Jeanne had draped a light sweater over her and led her into the fresh air, and she'd started to cry. And though Jeanne's voice was right by her, she'd understood nothing, her head had swirled with images mingled with salt, and she'd raised her head and looked up at the sky. But there was nothing to see, it was already late, a dark summer night, and there were no clouds at all. That made her start crying again, because a sky without clouds was a tragic thing, something that never should happen. She'd sobbed loudly, then André had come and hugged her, smothered her in kisses and led her back to her party. Carried her, almost like a trophy.

"You're not going to start crying again, are you?"

Dora shakes her head, but without conviction. Her head is full of voices.

"Good, because I have something important to say."

Was his head full of voices, too?

"Can we leave the others for a little bit?"

No, she doesn't think so. One voice, and endless rows of numbers, that's all that fills André's head. Maybe it was better that way. She laughs loudly at the thought, as if she were drunk. And he's already herding her into the other room, and she waves and smiles at people who cross her path. Father with two glasses, one full, one empty; Mother with newly acquired stylish red hair; Marc, who at the beginning of the evening had promised to write a play just for her, and had given her such an intense, earnest look that she'd felt a little queasy, and thought again how lucky it was that his eyes weren't green; then a friend of the family and his wife, who grins at her; then an old lady she doesn't know who turns her back on her . . . And then she is already in the adjoining room, where there is nothing but a narrow bed and a chair that must have looked impressive once, and a pile of light jackets and silk shawls: The summer nights in Paris can get chilly, you never know.

"Dora, marry me!"

Did André really shout the words, or did it just sound that way to her? He rarely shouts. Now that she stops to think about it, she'd never actually heard him raise his voice. Not ever.

"Be my wife!"

And before she can check herself, she asks, "Why?" At this moment, no word in the world could have been worse. André's head sinks slowly but inexorably, and as Dora tries to call up placating sentences from Antigone and Sophocles to her aid, he leaves the room. He does not run, he does not even increase his pace, yet somehow, Dora finds it impossible to detain him, she cannot reach him; and when she extends an arm toward him, it's as if she were reaching across the centuries. He's gone. On her big night. Dora thinks she'll never forgive him, though she's not sure. His timing couldn't have been worse. How could he have proposed tonight, of all nights? On a night when everything seems possible, when everything is opening up for her, when everything is truly getting started, for the first time.

She looks out the window. Still no clouds. That's also something she can't forgive the sky, or maybe André. Of that she's absolutely sure.

Luka tries to slip out of the room, not wanting to wake the woman. He doesn't know her name, but that doesn't bother him. It was just like yesterday, and the day before that, and the night before that; and so it had been for years. Maja, Ivana, Anita, Asija, Vera, Branka . . . A forest of names that summoned only the memory of a female form, and seldom the desire for a repeat encounter. Like a bag of Gummi Bears. Even if the colors and tastes are different, it makes no difference. And besides, he doesn't even like Gummi Bears!

Luka carefully pulls on his pants, and doesn't even bother to button his shirt, he's in a hurry. Luckily, it's summer, so a guy doesn't have a lot of clothes to put on, it takes little time to get dressed or undressed. Less time for a woman. All she's got to do is pull off her dress. Luka grins. He goes to the bathroom, and tries to make as little noise as possible as he pees. The mirror over the washbasin doesn't flatter him. His black hair is really too long, and his eyes may still be green, but they're red-rimmed and sleepy. Sure, it had been fun. Hello and good-bye. Actually, the woman from last night wasn't bad, maybe it'd be worth it to get her name, her number, something. Luka grins again. Same difference. Nothing makes a difference. He leaves the bathroom and the apartment and walks down the stairs with a light step. The night isn't so dark anymore. Suddenly he feels a yearning, an impatient, unsettled feeling. Today he's driving to Makarska. Going home.

The telephone rings. Dora is a plucky girl, her mother has always said. Bold and decisive, pure and simple. So she picks up right away.

"*Oui?*"

"It's me."

Obviously. Who else!

"André."

Yes, and?

Long silence.

"Dora, are you still there?"

"Yes."

"I want to talk to you."

That's your problem.

"Can I come over?"

Of course you would want to.

"There's something wrong with the connection. Dora, are you still there?"

"Yes."

"So, can I come over now?"

"Okay."

"I'll be right there. And, Dora . . ."

"What?"

"Nothing. I'll be right there."

Dora puts down the receiver. It's 9:52 in the morning. It's still very early. From the window of her little apartment in the Rue de Médicis, Dora's eyes rest on the Jardin du Luxembourg, and she breathes deeply, in and out. She loves this apartment, and the park with its puppet theater, which she visits so often that she knows all the plays and all the roles by heart. She loves this whole neighborhood, where everything that's important to her is concentrated in one place. She had wanted to live here for the longest time, and her father has made it possible: He gives her half the rent. But Dora is sure that won't be necessary for much longer, now that she will really start working and earning money. She smiles. The early morning hours do her good. She feels great. And André's visit can't change that.

The bus rounds the bend, and Luka sees the city in front of him. Only about fifteen minutes more and he'll be in Makarska. It's been months since he was here. The sea. He misses the sea. Painfully. It's easier to breathe when the sea is near. How much longer can he bear this separation? With the exhibition in Paris in October, it will be even harder. But he's going to leave Zagreb. It's already practically a decision. Not that he's so strong in that department. But this here, this feels like a decision. Because returning to Makarska isn't really a decision, it's a necessity. There's no alternative. It feels like he has no choice in the matter. And he likes that. Makarska is his home. It always has been. Where everything comes together. Makes sense. Has meaning. And the sea. There's no question of his staying in Paris after the exhibition ends, not even for a little while. Christian will probably try to persuade him to stay, yes, but there's no chance. Paris is great, a matchless place for a young artist, no question. An opportunity like this one presents itself only rarely. He's excited, he's gotten nearly everything ready, and who knows, maybe he'll even produce a couple of new paintings for the show. He has a truly immense desire to paint. Maybe it's because everything has become so clear to him, and so sudden, apparently. Or is it just the exhaustion and sleep deprivation talking? No. It can't be.

Luka leans back in his seat and closes his eyes. It's not worth it to fall asleep, he's almost there. He can rent a small studio. There must be dozens of empty garrets awaiting him. And women all over the place. Who can resist an up-and-coming young artist? Everything is coming together. After the Paris exhibition, he'll go back to the sea.

The bus enters the city, and if Luka's eyes were open, he would see the bus station. And Klara.

"I'm sorry, I understand, it was just absolutely terrible timing, I know; and I don't know what made me think of doing it then, you've got to believe me, you've just got to believe me . . ."

Dora is taken aback, but doesn't want to show it, because she herself doesn't know what she wants to do, or how things stand with André. Not a lot has happened since yesterday, but she's thought a lot. No, she actually didn't think at all. She just knew. Knew that there are other things and other people. Other men. And that there are some things you couldn't think away, and glances and facial expressions you couldn't retract, that could haunt you and never leave you in peace until everything is over, and you ask yourself what happened, even though you sensed what it was all along. That's what could happen, if she let it. Be that as it may, very soon she has to go to rehearsal. She's a professional actress now, with obligations and auditions and a fantastic role to study, and she can't let herself be distracted, she mustn't—now, when she's at the beginning, in the thick of everything, and already has had some success, and her head can juggle multiple voices very well, and she's not afraid anymore, just like her mother always said. She's just twenty-two, and she can do—or not do—whatever she wants, and marry whenever, and whomever, she wants. Or not. Everything is open to her, and she wants to be free, not to be pressured. André is kind and good-natured, and she loves him, certainly she does, in a way, but not in the right way. And what does it matter that they've been together four years already when everything is still possible and life is so full of surprises . . .

"Klara?!"

Klara nods and smiles a little, as if she were happy that Luka recognized her. Her hair is lighter, her body is much thinner, and she looks older than twenty-eight, as if she'd suffered some ordeal. As if she'd been sick. For a long time.

But of course Luka recognizes her. He'd gotten her pregnant, and hadn't wanted the baby. And she'd done what she knew he wanted her to do, without him having to say it. And then he was gone. Disappeared. Didn't get in touch, left her without a word. Abandoned himself and everything else. Was ashamed of himself, despised himself, but that didn't change anything. He went away. And then she went away, too, moved back to Makarska, the place that was home to her and to him, too—strange, that they should have met in Zagreb, that had always bothered him, as if the fact that they came from the same roots had divided them instead of uniting them—but now he's standing here and she's standing in front of him as if nothing had happened, and what is she doing at the bus station, anyway, and how did she know he was coming, and when he would arrive?

"What are you saying, Dorrie?"

André says "Dorrie" the way her mother used to when she was a kid, the way she still sometimes does, especially when she wants something from her. Dora has no idea what André is talking about, or what he expects of her. So she smiles at him shyly and intends to ask what he is talking about, when André passionately embraces her and whispers, *"I love you, I love you,"* in her hair. As if something had been decided. While she was away.

"Ana told me you were coming today." Then another smile.

All at once, Luka feels so indescribably tired that all he can do is smile back. It's a short and weak smile, but a smile nonetheless. He yearns for his bed, for a good, long, deep sleep. He wants to be alone. He gets his bag from the baggage compartment of the smelly bus, and goes on his way. Klara walks beside him, and her right arm, which is bare—it's summer—brushes every now and then against his, which is not as bare as hers. And so they walk, alongside each other, as if they belonged together, as if they would belong together even if they hadn't seen each other for years. Even if those years spent apart exceeded those they spent together.

Luka's bag is old and dark blue, and has survived many bus trips, but Luka isn't ashamed of it, he hasn't hidden it inside a plastic bag. He doesn't want to have to hide anything ever again.

Klara's hand touches his arm, and, suddenly, there it is, back in his life, against his will. The past. That he'd thought was over.

Chapter 9

Luka sees the young woman who's just walked in. She has black hair, long and wavy. And shiny. Like the glittering blue-black scales of a mackerel, a fish that must keep in constant motion or it will sink—it has something to do with its not having a swim bladder, Luka doesn't know for sure. This tall, slender woman is just like that—full of movement, even when she doesn't move, and he can't take his eyes off her. He's afraid she'll sink if he does.

Dora enters the gallery that her good friend Christian owns, and looks around expectantly. She has no invitation and doesn't know what she's about to see. A tall young man stands at the makeshift bar, staring at her. That doesn't bother Dora. She takes off her jacket. She doesn't want André to fuss over her while the tall young man is watching. "What's going on, Dora?" André asks. Ever since the proposal, she feels like he's constantly watching her, like he doesn't trust her. "Dora, what's going on?" he repeats. Dora says nothing and shakes her head, which suddenly starts to swim. It feels full and hollow, and blown up like a balloon, and hot and light and fluttery and transparent. She closes her eyes. She stands still, and stays that way, as images wash over her in waves. They almost pull her under. "Dorrie, what's going on?" André asks for the third time. He's impatient now.

Luka doesn't move. He leans against the bar and holds his breath. He's afraid that if he relaxes his muscles and breathes, the young woman will vanish. He fixates on her until it hurts and his eyes begin tearing up. Then his consciousness melts away and he slides to the floor. He doesn't have time to count, not even once. Slowly he slips away. Like images in an art catalog whose pages he slowly flips through.

Dora is the first to come to the side of the man who fainted. She has seen this once before. She has witnessed it. And she knows what to do. So she crouches beside him, tinier than tiny. Her eyes widen, until her face, paler than pale, seems to be nothing but eyes. She bends her head over the unconscious young man, and, before Christian, who had invited her to this exhibition of the work of a "talented Croatian artist," can kneel at his other side and raise his legs, she kisses his pale red mouth. "Dora!" André calls out, aghast. No time for pet names!

Luka hears a soft voice next to his face. "You are my sleeping beauty, only mine, wake up, my prince, you are my prince, only mine . . ." Then other voices and words reach his ears, until, confused and weak, he opens his eyes and sees hers; she is smiling. His lips move without making a sound, he can say nothing, so he smiles faintly and shakily raises his arm, stretches his hand toward her face, touches her long, black hair, and she whispers once again very softly, so softly that only her lips move, and only he can hear it: "You are my prince."

Chapter 10

"I can hardly believe it."

"I've got to keep looking at you."

"And I at you."

"You are stunning."

"Your eyes. They have always followed me."

"I don't know what to say."

"Your paintings are magnificent!"

"Yes, they're good."

"Even back then, I thought your paintings were fantastic."

"We were still children, back then."

"And now, your own show in Paris!"

"That was sixteen years ago!"

Life exists only in this moment. Timeless. Dora knows it. Memory is a cocktail of what you've lived and what you've heard, with a slice of lemon perched on the sugared rim of the glass. You can only separate the ingredients with difficulty. But this man. This is Luka. Even back then he was an artist. He'd painted a portrait of her. He'd painted constantly. Dora can remember everything. Everything she thought she'd lost. It's Luka. A boy with a box full of colored pencils. And look at him now, with his own solo show in Paris. She sits across from him, but actually she is inside him. Deep inside. In the past. It's Luka!

"How are you?"

"I've become an actress."

"You have?"

"I'm playing Cordelia."

"Is that good?"

"It's fantastic."

"What should we do now?"

"I have no idea."

"Then, let's just keep on sitting here."

"Okay."

"Do you have time?"

"All the time in the world."

"And that man, standing there?"

"What man?"

"The one who won't stop watching you?"

"I don't know him."

"Are you sure?"

"I don't know any man over there."

"But . . ."

"Truffaut is dead."

"Who?"

"Truffaut."

"I don't know him."

"He died a few weeks ago."

"A friend of yours?"

Luka wants to reach out and touch Dora, her pale skin that shimmers exotically under the red glow of the bar, but he's afraid. His hand won't stop shaking. His fear is immense. Of what, he doesn't know. He's no longer afraid that she will sink to the ocean floor, that's for sure. But he wants her to stay where she is, looking at him, moving her lips, smiling, talking and asking him questions. While he rests his hand on her stomach. Maybe he's afraid that the man across the room will come up and take her away from him. Before he can get her dress off. But she doesn't know the man, she said so herself. She will always be there now, so beautiful, sitting there, smiling at him, talking to him. His body begins to react to her presence and he understands nothing. Though everything is completely clear.

"I'm afraid."

"Of what?"

"I don't know."

"Come on, tell me."

"Of the man over there."

"That's ridiculous."

"What if he comes over and takes you away from me?"

"He can't."

"Good, well, at least we've cleared that up."

"Yes."

Dora sees tears in his eyes and she smiles, because life is beautiful. Luka. That was the name! And everything makes sense. She has waited and he has come; a proper man now, no longer a nine-year-old boy waiting for his muscles to come in; no, he looks like someone you could never bear to let go, so that her hands grow damp, and now everything has come together, and life can begin. She can already feel his mouth on her skin, and her stomach flutters with the wild wing beats of thousands of pelicans—she'd just seen a nature documentary on television—and everything is clear, and she's glad that she turned André down. *"Non,"* she had told him, and he'd reassured her that there was no hurry, that he had time. And now everything is over, the waiting is over, no more secrets, and everything is coming together, and her premiere will happen in a few months, and Luka is here, looking so damned gorgeous, and life is thrilling. It was such a long time ago, and that is and is not true, and it was another life, and there is no other life, and it's so incredible and Luka is here. And she's not just damp anymore: She's drenched.

"Let's get out of here."

Chapter 11

Dora opens the door, and Luka enters her apartment. He takes a couple of steps, and she locks the door behind him. He turns around. Dora takes off her coat, hangs it up, but it falls off the hook, and she lets it lie in a heap on the floor. Their eyes can see nothing but each other. Dora takes a step toward him. Luka concentrates on his breathing. He counts. She lays her hands on his cheeks, her face is so close to his that Luka can hardly see it.

"Breathe," he hears, and obeys. "Breathe," he hears, and suddenly he feels as if he were flying. Like a seagull that hovers in the summer heat and glides over the sea without moving its wings, fearless and self-assured, carried by the wind.

Everything that happens next happens naturally and unselfconsciously, even though their teeth bump on first contact, and their noses collide as they seek their place. Even though they start laughing because their arms get all tangled, and their hands can't get at the skin underneath all their clothes fast enough—it's November—and even though they aren't quite sure where they are, or what is beneath them, it's a priceless, unbookable voyage out of Jules Verne, from which no traveler in his right mind would ever wish to return.

It's dark in the apartment. The only light comes from the street-lamps that cast their glow over the busy road below. But Dora and Luka navigate the darkness like cats with night vision, or like blind people who've learned over the years how to rely on their other senses.

Their lips are untiring. Their bodies are everywhere. Inseparable. An occasional twinge of pain only increases their desire for more skin. They will emerge with marks and bruises that they will wear like medals. With pride. Everything is new, and everything is for the first time, and despite this, everything feels completely right. Or because of this. Dora lets out a short, deep moan as Luka squeezes her more tightly in his arms. He clutches her like a life preserver.

"What is it?" she asks, gasping for air.

"We're grown up now."

"You could say so."

"And I . . ."

. . . love you only you always you my whole life long you are my breath my heartbeat you are infinite in me you are the sea that I see and the fish that I catch you have lured into my net you are my day and my night and the asphalt beneath my shoes and the tie around my neck and the skin on my body and the bones under my skin and my boat and my breakfast and my wine and my friends and my morning coffee and my paintings and my paintings and my wife in my heart and my wife my wife my wife my wife . . .

"What is it?"

"Nothing. My arm has fallen asleep."

"That's all right."

"What just happened?"

"I made love to you. An absolute stranger." And she laughs.

"Not all that strange."

"You're right. But that was a thousand years ago, when we were little kids, and we didn't know anything."

"Not true. I knew then everything that I know now. Everything."

"This, too?" Dora lifts her head and steals a curious sidelong glance at him, as she traces her fingers across his ribs. Luka gets goose bumps. "And that?" Her mouth is on his stomach, and before her tongue can reach him, Luka moans, and pushes her gently away.

"I love you." Life is so simple.

"And I love you." Life is so simple.

The darkness fades, and a gray, foggy November day dawns in Paris. And everyone has said, "I love you."

"So . . . what's the story with the man at the gallery?"

Chapter 12

Luka spends three months with Dora in Paris.

"I don't want to go," Luka says the morning after. Dora lies in his arms. The world is more than all right.

"Don't ever go away again." Dora's voice is dreamy, trailing off into his shoulder.

"*I* never went away."

"That one time doesn't count, I was still a kid, I had no choice." She could fall asleep at any second.

"Maybe, but I stayed, all the same, and you were gone, and *that* should never happen again."

"All right, agreed. But I don't ever want you to go away, even if you never did before." Her voice is barely audible.

"Okay."

"Wonderful."

"And how do we make that happen? What do we do now?" His voice is much more awake than hers.

"Sleep." No sooner said than done.

. . .

Luka lives with Dora.

"I like your apartment, it's so big and warm. And it smells so good here." Luka walks around the rooms, hands in his pockets, touching everything with his gaze.

"It's just me, my place smells of me. Of me with you." Dora follows him, slides her hands into his pockets. "But big? It's only a student apartment."

Luka laughs.

"What?"

"You have no idea what a student apartment looks like, and how many people could live in a place like this." He turns around and looks at her, his eyes are full of tenderness. Or even admiration. As if her cluelessness were something precious and unique.

Luka sleeps in Dora's bed.

The bed is in the traditional French style, designed for one and a half people. Luka doesn't understand the point of this. What is "one and a half," what kind of a person is that supposed to be?! But it's cozy, and at least it means that there's no way to keep their bodies from touching all night long.

"I've never been able to fall asleep with someone like this, hugging and holding each other tight. I couldn't stand feeling someone's breath on my neck."

"You've become a new man, in record time." She smiles and kisses him.

"No, I've finally become the person I used to be, the person I've always been inside. But without you . . ."

"Yes, remember this: Without me there's only the dot-dot-dot."
They look at each other, and everything is clear.

Sometimes Luka wakes in Dora's bed unsure where he is. He
thinks he's still in Zagreb, next to some woman he'd met the night
before; but then his nose awakens and he smells Dora, her hair that
smells of the theater, and her rose-scented skin—it's her night cream,
she says an actress has to pay more attention to her appearance than
other women do—and all of this happens in a matter of seconds, and
then he reaches for her and holds her; sometimes, still dreaming, she
murmurs incomprehensible words to him or some other visitor in her
dreams, other times she caresses him, and they make love, half asleep,
with half-closed eyes.

Luka eats in Dora's small dining room.

"This is delicious," Luka says, taking seconds.

"Yes, I can cook well, when I feel like it." Dora's mouth is full, and
they laugh.

They laugh a lot. Never have two people laughed so much together.

"But what's it called?"

"I came up with it myself."

"Still, it must have a name."

"Why? Do all your paintings have names?"

"Naturally. Without a name, it doesn't work, they wouldn't sell."

"But I have no plans to sell my culinary creations!" And they start
laughing again, and so it goes, on and on, and they can't stop laughing. As if their heads and hearts were six and nine years old again. At
the most.

"That has nothing to do with it! What if tomorrow my fans and patrons, and all the journalists who incessantly hound me, demand to know what my favorite meal is? What will I tell them? Oh, you know, there's this dish, with a lot of vegetables and goat cheese, with rice added in, and the sauce is really dark—probably tomatoes and red wine . . ." Luka makes funny faces as he says this and they laugh.

"Oh, all right, if you insist, then I will dub this dish that has no receipe 'Lukazzoni,' spelled with a *k*, to be sure." She bows and he applauds, and they're happy, happier than they were back then, when she was six and he was nine.

Luka goes with Dora on long walks through the city.

Every day she draws up a short route and they dress warmly before heading out, the first snow has fallen already, but they brave the cold with red noses and frozen jaws. That puts an end to the laughter! The cold stings their noses so sharply that they can scarcely bear to breathe. Which of course could be a problem. So they rub each other's ears and blow warm breaths into each other's faces. Dora keeps on trying to burrow into Luka's jacket, but that makes them stumble, and, more often than not, they land on the hard ground. Then they try to laugh but it doesn't work. Everything is frozen. Hard as stone. No feeling left. Over and done with. So they hurry home and seek refuge in the warmth.

But sometimes the sky isn't so gray, and the sun struggles through, and a couple of clouds push forward; then Dora and Luka look at each other conspiratorially, a little shy to have caught each other noticing.

"There, Rodin's *The Thinker*!"

"Ooh là là, how lofty we are, mademoiselle!"

"But that's what it is, look before the wind carries it off, or changes it!"

"Yes, for instance, into a cathedral whose bell tower has been smashed, probably by a bomb."

"You shouldn't make up stories like that, these are just shapes, not events in time! And a cathedral? Hardly. You can't just make things up, it's got to be right, otherwise, we wouldn't need clouds at all, you could just . . ."

"Now I'm remembering. It's just like back then."

"What do you mean, just like back then?"

"Whenever you don't get your way . . ."

"What do you mean, my way?"

". . . then you get upset and sob . . ."

"I'm not sobbing at all, I never cry!"

". . . or you get angry and want to quit playing with me."

"You're so childish, that's so stupid, I can't believe you actually think that!" Dora turns and walks away from him with quick steps, her head hanging low.

"Here we go again." He bursts out laughing and shouts after her, "Do you want to go swimming? To the rock?"

Luka lets Dora guide him through the city and explain everything.

First she shows him the cemetery of Montmartre. They spend countless hours there: Dora wants him to see the grave of every single famous person, most of whom he's never heard of, she can never get enough of those cold, gray stones. Her mouth is full of names that sound all the grander because of the way she pronounces them.

Then come the sights, so many of them, one after another, which are inexhaustible in Paris, as everyone knows: Paris seems to consist entirely of famous buildings and fascinating monuments. It's as if a historic event had occurred behind every door, and a famous person were born in every house! Luka gets tired even thinking about the next day and its secrets, which are not so secret, since they can be found in any, or at least in one, of the countless travel guides. Sometimes he wishes he could simply do nothing at all, just close his eyes and contemplate the images that arise in his own head. But in the end, he can't resist this matchless city, and, like Dora and millions of others before her, he succumbs to its charms. Though for him, its main attraction is that it's Dora's city.

Luka waits for Dora while she's at the theater.

Sometimes he has to let her head out on her own, giving her a kiss, one last tentative hug, stroking her hair and looking at her one last time as she disappears out the apartment door, or into the theater building when he accompanies her there. And then his life comes almost to a halt. He's left with nothing to do but to continually check the time, which always seems to stand still.

He could use this time to call his father, or Ana, for example. To tell them what's going on. But he doesn't want to. More than anything, he doesn't want to think about why he isn't calling. He'd rather look at the clock, which—yet again—seems definitely to have stopped.

But one day, amid these hours of overflowing solitude, he discovers someone who makes it possible for him to forget about the waiting. Pablo Neruda. Luka had never heard of him, but he finds two books of his poems on Dora's bookshelf: *The Captain's Verses* and *100 Love Sonnets*. Luka has never been drawn to poetry before. He's never been able to work up any enthusiasm for it. But these poems land on him like the sirocco, Croatia's warm, rainy southern wind that makes it hard to breathe. And yet, you can't resist it. Again and again, you turn your head into the wind, and let it caress and enfold you. *Take away my bread, if you wish, / take away my breath, but / leave me your laughter.* Poetry can be so easy. He'd never known. *My love, / we found each other / thirsty and we / drank up all the water and the blood, / we found each other / hungry / and we bit one another / as the fire bites, / leaving wounds behind.* So easy to understand, so clear. *But / if every day, / every hour / you feel that you are destined for me / with implacable sweetness. / If every day / a flower rises to your lips to seek me, / oh my love, oh my own, / all that fire endures in me still, / in me nothing is extinguished or forgotten, / my love feeds on your love, beloved, / and while you live it will remain in your arms / without leaving mine.* Luka is a million percent sure that Neruda must have known about Luka and Dora, and wrote these verses only for them. He wants to learn Spanish. He has to be able to read these words in Neruda's language. He can hardly wait for Dora to come home so they can read the poems aloud to each other. Like a never-ending conversation.

Luka helps Dora learn her lines.

And Dora weeps with laughter.

"You can't do it, you can't speak French at all!" She covers his mouth with kisses, every laugh line, every crevice.

"I can, too; listen!" And again he produces a string of sounds that mean nothing and never will; he practically sings in his struggle to sound French. And Dora weeps with laughter.

"That was right, wasn't it?"

Dora looks at him lovingly and strokes his face.

"In any case, I don't have to know how to speak French, I just have to be able to follow your words, so I can give you a cue if you need prompting." He stares fixedly at the incomprehensible text in front of him, a deep furrow forming between his brows.

"Good. So, what are you waiting for, let's be off, *mon capitaine!* And don't be harsh with me if I forget a word."

"You'll see, I'm merciless! The punishment will be terrible, watch out!" And what do they end up doing? Laughing, of course. Laughter is like an incurable disease with them.

Luka visits Dora at rehearsals.

Yes, sometimes he's permitted. Then he sits in the empty theater, way in back, almost in the last row, and listens to her. It feels like a reward to him, even though he understands hardly anything. He can figure out what's happening onstage, more or less, but he doesn't understand what the actors are saying. But that doesn't bother him because he comes to watch Dora, to listen to her, to marvel at her, even to get a little jealous of the old king who gets to hold her in his arms for such a long time at the end. Jealousy is a new emotion for Luka, especially jealousy over a woman. But he still remembers Dora's first day of kindergarten, and her divine, incomparable, flawless bag that he couldn't get enough of. Back then, he was jealous. Or maybe it was more like envy. Yes, he had just wanted that bag; it hadn't mattered that it was Dora's. But now it even bothers him that the old man onstage gets to touch her—that he has to touch her, in fact! It's part of their job. He swallows hard. What comes next? Kissing, caresses, nude scenes? All at once, he feels sick and has to rush to the men's bathroom, to splash water on his face. He bathes his eyes with cold water, rinsing away the images. That exist only in his mind.

"So, how was it? How was I? Did you like it?"

His answer is a long silence. Until he takes her in his arms and holds her tight.

"I love you, too, my only love."

With Christian's help, Luka finds a small studio to sublet, and paints for many hours each day.

Yes, he manages to paint, it makes him extremely happy. But he does it only when Dora is busy, when she doesn't have time for him. And maybe because it's only rarely that Dora has no time for him, he paints quickly, very quickly. He's never painted so quickly before. He could paint with his eyes closed, the pictures come to him so effortlessly—as if they were photographs, as if he had only to press a button and out they came. This new way of filling canvases with color delights him. It comes as a huge surprise, and Luka lets himself be surprised; when he contemplates each finished painting, he feels as if he's never seen anything like it before, something indescribable takes form before his eyes, brought into being by his priming brush, his flat brush, his sable brush and his round brush, and even if Luka doesn't always know what it is, he knows that it's good, very good, even. Like his new life. He knows that, at this moment, he is everything he could ever be.

With Christian's help, Luka sells two paintings.

But his heart is heavy: They are his two favorites. His heart beats faster when he looks at them. He had wanted to give one of them to Dora as a present. But the buyer wants exactly those two, and Luka gives his consent because he needs the money, for himself, for Dora and for everything that's to come: A lot is about to happen, he can feel it, and he wants to be ready, they can't be short of money, nothing should go wrong just because they don't have enough money, absolutely, positively not. He's confident that he can sell all his paintings in Paris, and enlists Christian to help him.

"Nothing should be left before we go back to the sea, sell everything!"

Christian is taken aback, he raises his eyebrows questioningly—he's plucked them into a thin line, something he did on a senseless, childish dare—the kind of stunt that only unmarried middle-aged men would do.

"Dora is leaving Paris?"

"Sure, after the premiere, if she . . . I don't know. I think so." He looks at his friend uncertainly, hoping for agreement. "What do you mean? Isn't she coming with me?"

"I don't know. But I can't imagine it." His frankness hits Luka like a quart of black paint. He starts counting. But Christian is there, and by now he knows a bit about Luka's fainting spells. He lays his hand on his arm.

"Just keep painting, everything will turn out for the best."

So Luka paints, and Christian sells, and Dora is overjoyed.

Luka goes to galleries and museums.

Sometimes alone, sometimes with Dora. Dora is well acquainted with them. They spend hours in the Louvre, almost every day. They sit or stand silently in front of masterpieces of every era. Any word at all would be one word too many. Mostly they go to the Musée de l'Orangerie, which has been renovated and newly reopened this year, to see the Impressionist and Post-Impressionist paintings in the collection of Jean Walter and Paul Guillaume, they can't get enough of them. All these names! Luka knows them all, they're like old friends, he feels as if they had guided him through his life, stood beside him, shaped his vision. Luka is almost ecstatic. The pressure of his hand hurts Dora, but she says nothing. She knows what it means to be rendered deaf, dumb and blind with emotion. Dazzled. Possessed. Driven by passion.

"I'm one of them," Luka says quietly. "I'm one of them."

Luka eats with Dora at cozy little restaurants with excellent food.

It's an art, this food. It reminds him of his paintings, of the special mixtures of color that sometimes arise by accident, which turn out to be unforgettable. He tries everything, he's curious. But when he tries to do the ordering, the waiters either grin and smile at him or (depending on the type of restaurant) take offense at his pronunciation of their menu offerings: It sounds pretty French—Luka is musical and he's been in town for a while now!—but what he's saying means nothing, absolutely nothing. He would starve if Dora weren't there, it's come to that.

"What would I do without you?"

"Die."

And everything is clear to everyone.

Dora gives him Neruda poems in Spanish.

Luka gets to know Dora's best friend, Jeanne.

And Papou, naturally. The four of them go walking in the Parc Monceau. The young women tell him funny stories about their childhood and laugh a lot, and Luka envies them, and wishes he could have been there. And though Papou is very old by now and moves stiffly, Luka can picture how wild and unruly he must have been in his prime. Images arise in his head, some of them reappear later in his studio as portraits. He gives one of them to Jeanne, the other to Dora.

"Dora never spoke of you. And I'm her best friend!"

"I'd simply forgotten him." Dora isn't lying. She looks at him with love as she says it.

"You didn't want to remember me," Luka corrects her.

"I don't understand it." Jeanne is sitting between the two of them in a café, looking from one of them to the other.

"It would have been too painful to think about him. I thought I wouldn't survive it. So I forgot about him." Dora's voice breaks, and Luka looks at her with concern.

"But I'm here now. To stay." He reaches his arm across the table and strokes her cheek, and Dora rests her face in his hand. She closes her eyes. A smile floats across her full lips, like a light breeze.

"What a crazy story." Jeanne groans, and orders another glass of wine. Oh, why not a bottle! For everyone.

Luka goes with Dora to see her mother.

"No, I can't believe it!!! It's like in a novel! I'd publish it anytime. But I would have recognized you all the same, yes, really. You can still see the little boy in you, in your eyes, especially in your eyes. They remind me of someone, Dora, who do his eyes remind me of, so green, such a deep, bright green? Dora, what do you think? And your paintings, simply fantastic, pure and simple, out of this world! What would you say to a small monograph on your work? I could do it. Really, I just can't believe it. After so many years, that doesn't happen every day. Kids, take note—this is something unique. Soul mates, Marc called it when I told him about it, you've absolutely got to meet him, Luka, you'll get along brilliantly, after all, you're both artists!

Dora, just imagine, you're all artists! I'm so happy to see you again. When I think of how it was back then, and how inseparable the two of you were, like two overcooked noodles, stuck together. It was adorable. We must meet again sometime and do things together. I'm so happy you've found each other again. It's the way it ought to be. Pure and simple. Back then I thought . . . but no, let's not talk about that—now when everything has fallen so nicely into place. Yes, my Dorrie, it wasn't easy, back then . . ."

Luka goes with Dora to see her father.

After Ivan has drunk his second Cognac, he smiles nervously.

"So, you two have a pretty unusual history." He pours himself a third glass. He's generous with the precious liquid. "Sure you won't have one?" He nods at the bottle.

"No, thanks. I only drink wine, but not now. I don't want to embarrass myself in front of you . . ." Luka smiles, he's also a little nervous. He fumbles for Dora's hand and presses it lightly. She's there. Good.

"So what's your next step? What are your plans?" Ivan sinks back into his old armchair, the one that was brand-new and highly fashionable sixteen years ago. Today it's neither one nor the other. And Dora sees that the chair suits her father, and it pains her.

"I don't know." Luka looks at Dora and smiles. "We haven't talked about it yet." And Dora smiles back at him. If they weren't so deeply in love, all this smiling could get a little annoying.

"Ask us something easier, Dad." Dora makes an effort not to get sad when she's with her father. She tries to cover up her feelings of desolation, she can do that, of course, it's her métier. Luka knows that. But she wouldn't win a Palme d'Or for this performance.

"How long are you staying in Paris?" Ivan looks at the two of them as if to say, Is that question easy enough for you?

Dora laughs, stands up and gives him a kiss on the cheek. Luka shakes his head, and his glance falls on the white carpet, which is marked with many stains.

"And what's your opinion on the toxic gas catastrophe in India? Four thousand five hundred killed, hard to imagine!"

And Luka loves Dora.

With his whole life. He can't compare this love to anything else. To anything else he knows. He thinks of the small boy and his best friend, back then, back when he still didn't know that people could disappear, just like that. Even though they give warning. That doesn't change anything. They're gone. They don't exist anymore. Did he think, back then, that he would ever see her again? He doesn't know. But now she's here, and he's here, too, and everything's fallen into place. Because Dora loves him. And he loves Dora. *Before I loved you, my love, nothing was mine: / I floated among streets and things: / Nothing counted, nothing had a name: / The world was made of expectant air.* Dora's smiling tears are his bread and his water. It wouldn't surprise him if he himself were to start writing poetry. But what for? Nobody can do it better than Neruda. Everything has already been said. You should never try to improve something that has already attained perfection.

Luka is happy. As happy as one has to be in order to be happy. Luka doesn't think of Makarska. Almost everything he desires and needs is right here beside him. Only the sea is missing.

A few weeks after the show, Luka calls his father.

"Papa, it's me." And then an awkward silence.

"Luka, my son, how are you? Is everything okay?" Zoran's calm voice.

"Everything's great, no worries."

"Good."

"And how are you?"

"Great."

"What's going on at the hotel?"

"Not a whole lot. But nearly a hundred people are coming for New Year's Eve, they want to celebrate it here."

"Well, that's good."

"Yes."

"For business."

"Sure."

"Have you gone fishing?"

"Yes, last weekend."

"And?"

"Not good. Not good."

"That's how it is, sometimes."

"Yeah, I know."

"So, then."

"See you soon, son."

Luka calls Makarska only one more time. To talk to Ana. A totally different story.

"It's me."

"Luka, where are you? What are you doing? When are you coming back?" She's excited, but words don't fail her. No, not her.

"I don't know."

"What's happened? Where are you hiding?"

"I'm still in Paris."

"What are you doing there? You said you'd come back two weeks ago, at most." It's almost an accusation.

"I know."

"What do you mean, you know? Just come home!"

"We'll see."

"And what does *that* mean?"

"I'll get in touch later."

"You should get in touch with Klara. She doesn't complain, but she's crazy with worry. You can't just disappear like this . . ."

"I'll get back in touch later."

"Luka, what's wrong? What's going on?"

"I can't tell you on the phone."

"Then, come home! This just isn't right!"

"Everything's fine, Ana. Really."

"It doesn't sound like it."

"I'll be in touch."

"Don't forget to call Klara."

"Talk to you soon, Ana."

He doesn't call Klara. Of course not. There's no Klara. Klara is from another life, not his life. His life is Dora. But no word yet to the others about Dora. He wants to keep her to himself as long as possible.

Throughout this time, he loves her. Passionately. Unconditionally. Completely.

Chapter 13

That man from the gallery calls the morning after. Many times. Dora can tell it's him from the urgency of the ring tone. Hurried. Impatient. Insistent. Only numbers in his head. She knows she's not being fair, it's not really true. All the same, she doesn't answer. She absolutely will not go to the phone, because Luka is there, and she's got better things to do. She's taking a crash course in growing up. She smiles at the thought. Dora is happy. She's not going to talk on the phone. Not now. Never, if she got her way. But she knows that's not possible. Some other time, just not now. So the telephone rings all day long.

"Is that the man from the gallery?" Luka asks.

"Maybe." Her voice says, "I don't want to talk about it."

And so the day after passes.

The day after the day after is already some other time. At exactly 8:15, Dora sits down on the couch by the phone and dials the number she's known by heart for years. She's chosen exactly the right moment to call, the time when André will be rushing to get ready for work and leave his apartment. She's thought everything through. His phone rings. Dora feels a little nervous, she's never done something like this before. It keeps ringing. No time for a big discussion. Just arranging a time to meet. It's ringing. No explanations. It's ringing. No questions and answers. It's ringing. Just arranging a time to meet. It's . . .

"*Oui?*"

"It's me."

Silence.

"Dora."

"I know."

"Can we meet up?"

"Why?"

"There's something I want to tell you."

"Can't you do it over the phone?"

"I'd rather not."

"As you like."

"Can it be today?"

"You're in a hurry."

Silence.

"All right."

"I could come to your place."

"To my place?"

"Or we could meet at the station."

"The station?"

"You decide."

"Why don't we meet at Chez Alfredo?"

"I don't want to eat."

"At Club Jazz, then."

Silence. As if she were mulling it over.

"No. Let's meet at Café Blanche."

"But we've never gone there before."

"Exactly."

Silence.

"I get it."

"At five?"

"That's too early. I have a meeting at four."

"Good, then, at six?"

"Okay."

"Till then."

"Till then."

Dora and Luka make a show of embracing at the door. Even though nobody's there to see them. He kisses her on both cheeks, gallantly. Her eyes are wide, and her forehead looks contemplative. Then they kiss on the mouth, and she leaves. Her departing back tells Luka clearly and plainly, "I know what I'm doing. Everything's going to be fine."

André is already sitting at a corner table. He doesn't look good. It hurts Dora to see him like this. He stands up. At first he smiles at her—looking at her always makes him happy—but then his face suddenly grows pale and masklike. He knows what they've come here for. Of course he knows. In a café where they are meeting for the first time, and probably the last. Before Dora sits down, she gently touches his face. That is, she wants to touch it. But he leans back, and her hand remains in the air, unsupported. Abandoned. She will have to accept that. There's no way around it.

"André, I'm leaving you."

"What?" What she's saying comes as no surprise. It's the immediacy with which she says it that unnerves him.

"I'm leaving you."

"Why?"

"It's the only fair thing to do."

"Fair to who?"

"To me and to you."

"But I love you."

"Yes, I know." Dora finds it hard to look him in the eye.

"So, then, why?"

"I do like you, too."

"You like me? You *like* me?" His voice grows markedly too loud.

"Yes, and you know that." Dora softens her voice.

"What about love? Do you love me?"

"I don't know."

"After four years, you don't know."

"That's why we should break up."

André is quiet for a while. He ponders, and looks at her suspiciously. As if he can't quite follow her logic. Suddenly his face brightens.

"You had a one-night stand, you enjoyed it, and now you think you have to leave me. But that's not the case. It doesn't matter to me. I can deal with it. I proposed to you, maybe you remember. Forever and ever. I love you."

"Forever and ever." Dora repeats the words as if she were in a trance. Then she says in an unexpectedly loud voice, "I love somebody else."

"After one night?"

Dora is silent. She doesn't want to explain anything.

"My God, women are so stupid! After one night? He was that good? What did he do? Magic?"

Dora stays silent. It would be senseless to say anything. Forever and ever. That's all that counts.

"Do you even know his name? Or did the two of you not have time for such trivialities?"

"Luka." The answer comes automatically, as if she couldn't suppress it, couldn't deny it. Especially not now, when she's just found him again.

"Luka? The artist? From the show? It was him?" He stares at her in disbelief, but then starts laughing, too loudly. "Of course, you run off with the leading man."

"His name is Luka." Dora is lost in thought, her smile distracted and dreamy. She's dived into the waves of the Mediterranean. But André can't see that. Nobody could. It's her own private performance. A kind of monologue.

"And you love him? Just like that, overnight?" André swallows audibly, as if he were choking on his thoughts. "Literally overnight."

"No."

"Since when, then?"

"My whole life."

André looks at her uncomprehendingly.

"Literally." Dora's face glistens like a figure skater's short dress.

André falls silent.

"My Luka." Finally she can look at André with a clear conscience.

"My Luka." She can't hide the glee in her voice. Her joy has over-powered her desire to spare André's feelings, to hurt him as little as possible.

"'My,' like 'My Prince Charming'?" He doesn't manage to make it sound as mocking as he means it to. Because his shock is so genuine.

"Yes, my Prince Charming."

Chapter 14

It's been decided. With very few tears, and only three fainting spells, none of them with dire consequences. There are still things to take care of. People to tell. Preparations to make. But soon enough, they'll be back together again. It's been decided. They still have to decide where and when, but there are telephones, thank God. They smile at each other in the darkness of the bedroom where they can't stop making love. It's been decided. Luka calls his father and gives him the details. Zoran sounds happy. Dora stands nearby, smiling weakly. Zoran's gain is her loss. It's been decided. Dora doesn't feel like she's going to die. Not yet. Because Luka's still there, she can touch him. He can make love to her. Fulfill her, and her life.

At the train station, a cold wind blows. It's the beginning of February, and it's snowing again, but Dora and Luka don't care. The Four Horsemen of the Apocalypse could charge past them on the platform and they wouldn't notice. How does it go, that song about saying good-bye? When someone you love goes away . . . Better not think about that. Everything has already been said. Dora doesn't cry, and Luka doesn't faint. Everything is wonderful. Organized.

"I'm glad you're taking the train."

"Why?"

"That way it will take you longer to leave me. It gives us more time." Dora kisses his soft, cold mouth.

"*Me falta tiempo para celebrar tus cabellos.*" Luka holds Dora's face in his hands and smiles at her. They've promised each other to be brave.

"I wonder if you really have any idea what you're saying, or if you've just memorized it all." Her face trembles in his hands.

"Test me."

"All right, tell me what it means."

"*I could never have enough time to celebrate your hair.*" He looks at her, obviously pleased with himself.

"Not bad. But that wasn't a hard one. Tell me another," she challenges him.

"You can't be serious. You want to challenge me, the supreme Neruda expert? Outrageous. You brazen upstart."

"Is that supposed to be Neruda?" Dora draws down the corners of her mouth. "Weak, my love, very weak."

"*Amo el trozo de tierra que tú eres, / porque de las praderas planetarias / otra estrella no tengo. Tú repites / la multiplicación del universo,*" he recites. People stare at him curiously as they pass.

"Not bad. That sounds for once like you know what you're saying." Dora is moved. She acts like it's nothing, but notices her words are no longer completely obeying her.

"Thank you. That's probably because I actually know what I'm saying: *I love the piece of earth that you are, / because in all the planetary prairies, / I have no other star. You multiply the universe.*"

Dora smiles. "Well, then. You'd better stick to your paints."

Then they both fall silent. People rush past them. Trains arrive and depart. It's loud and cold, and smells of stale air.

"That wasn't a good idea."

"Yes. Neruda isn't the life of the party."

"No. He makes me miss you. Even though you're standing right here in front of me."

"He wants me to stay here."

"Then stay."

"Dora."

"I know."

"We'll see each other again before you know it."

"Yes, I know."

"Don't cry."

"I won't cry if you don't start counting."

"What do you mean?"

"I see your lips, the way they're moving, and I see your eyes, already taking cover behind your eyelids."

"No, I'm looking at you. I can't afford not to look at you."

"Stay."

"Dora."

"I don't think I can take this."

"You didn't say good-bye to me either."

"When?"

"The time when I was sitting on our rock and waiting for you. You never came."

"I don't remember that very well."

"I hated you."

"I can't believe that."

"I wanted to be dead."

"I'm sure that I wanted to come see you. You were my one and only, and they took me away from you and there was nothing I could do about it. I was still so little, and all I could do was cry and hate my life. I lay in my bed, holding the portrait of me that you'd painted, and I kept thinking of you, and . . ." Dora can no longer speak. Luka has to hold her tight to keep her from sinking onto the dirty gray platform. "I'm remembering everything now. Everything. I know it again. It's all coming back, I can see it!" Her voice is weak in triumph.

Luka is fighting against the entire world. And with Dora's agitation. He almost can't hold her up any longer. It's a relief when she suddenly rights herself. But then she looks at him, horror-stricken. What does she see? Gradually, Luka gets scared.

"You're never coming back. You'll leave me now, and we'll never see each other again."

"Dora, there's only you and me, and now we're grown up, and nothing and nobody can keep us apart, or stop us from spending our lives together. That's the way it is, and that's how it always will be." Luka knows he doesn't have much more time: He's short of breath, everything that keeps him alive is draining from him. He feels his eyelids fall shut, and starts to count: one, two, three, four, five . . . and then Dora's kiss pulls him out of the darkness again. Everything happens quickly then, without a proper transition to make things easier.

To crown it all, the train is already there. Right on time. How often does that happen? Especially in France. What happened to those glorious times when you'd have to wait for the train for half an hour, or even a whole hour? But the train is there. It's two minutes until departure. There's hardly any time left, none to speak of. Luka stands on the steps.

"*El amor supo entonces que se llamaba amor. / Y cuando levanté mis ojos a tu nombre / tu corazón de pronto dispuso mi camino.* Sonnet seventy-three. You must look it up. It's the answer to everything. Remember it! You must remember it!"

The train departs.

The train has left the station and can't be seen anymore. Not even a harmless, tiny fleeing snake anymore. Vanished, as if it had never been there at all.

Dora lingers on the platform, motionless.

Luka.

She is afraid.

Chapter 15

It's a long journey. With many stops. Dora would like that, Luka thinks. He's slowly withdrawn from her. Whether he's on the train, in a station, or on a bus, he holds Neruda firmly in his hand. A life-sustaining umbilical cord. An elixir of life. A life preserver. All in one. The poems are a guarantee that everything they'd said, felt and experienced was true, that it hadn't just been a dream. That it can't vanish.

The bus rounds the bend, and Luka sees the city appear in front of him. Only about fifteen minutes more and he'll be in Makarska. It's been months since he was here. The sea. He misses the sea. Painfully. It's easier to breathe when the sea is near. He misses Dora. He can breathe only when Dora is with him. He closes his eyes and begins to count: one, two, three, four, five, six . . . He's already feeling the comfortable lightness of unconsciousness. . . . No, he must not give in to it, he promised Dora. That's all that counts. And she's counting on him. Everything has to be resolved quickly now. *I had hardly left you* . . . It's already practically a decision. Not that he's strong in that department, or ever has been, no. But this here, this feels like a decision. Because it really isn't a decision, it's a necessity. There is no alternative. It feels like he has no choice in the matter. And he likes that. That's the way he wants it to be. He's found his life again. Unexpectedly. And Dora is his home. Always has been. Where everything comes together. Makes sense. Has meaning. And the sea. It's clear. Everything has become so clear. Or is it just the exhaustion talking? Two days on the road, with hardly any sleep. No. It can't be that. Because several months ago, with one glance, everything became clear. With the first word. Even before the first word. Suddenly, unexpectedly, and yet primally, sealed with their first kiss.

Luka leans back in his seat and shuts his eyes. It's not worth it to fall asleep, he's almost there. Dora, *Where are you? I felt, deep within me, / between my necktie and my heart, and higher, / a melancholy in my ribs:/ it was the knowledge that you suddenly were gone.* Dora.

It's been decided. Before you know it, he promised her. Before you know it. Everything will come together and work out. He feels very tired.

The bus enters the city, and if Luka's eyes were open, he would see the bus station. And Klara.

"Klara?"

Klara nods, and smiles a little, as if she were happy that Luka recognized her. Her hair is longer, her body is more filled out, and she looks older than almost twenty-nine, as if she'd suffered some ordeal. As if she'd been sick. For a long time. Sick or unhappy or abandoned and forgotten.

But of course Luka recognizes her. Even though it's been a few months since he last saw her, last spoke to her, last had any sort of contact with her. He hasn't missed her, hasn't thought of her at all. Not once, not for the briefest moment, has she been a part of his life these last few months. But now he's standing here, and she's standing in front of him, as if these months of silence had never happened. What is she doing in the station, anyway, and how had she known that he was coming, and when . . .

"Ana told me you were coming sometime today." Then another smile. "This is the second bus I've waited for. I was going to wait for the next one, too."

And all at once, Luka feels so indescribably tired that all he can do is smile, even though it's a short, weak, noncommittal smile, like one you'd give a stranger, when you don't know what you're supposed to say, but still. He longs for his bed, for a good, solid sleep. He wants to be alone. He wants to call Dora. He needs to hear her voice immediately. He collects his two trunks from the baggage compartment of the smelly bus and goes on his way. Klara walks beside him, and her right arm, encased in the thick sleeve of her coat—it's February— brushes every now and then against his, which is just as thickly cloaked. And so they walk, alongside each other, as if they belonged together, even though they haven't seen each other for months. The time they've spent apart exceeds the time they've spent together. And even when they were together, they hadn't been truly together, just sort of together. He hadn't seen them as committed, they'd slept together a few times, but there had always been other women, they'd gone to the movies a few times, or gone out on the boat. But nothing serious, it was all just for fun. There'd never been any promises, nothing like that. And Klara hadn't protested. Not once had she asked him if he loved her. He'd never asked her what she wanted from him, after all they'd been through, and how badly he'd treated her at the end. It hadn't interested him. To him, Klara was just one of many. In these irresistibly chaotic years of waiting that had felt like they could have gone on forever. But, thank God, Dora is not Godot. She came back. Dora. He must hear her voice at once.

Klara's hand touches his arm, as if to stop him from walking, and suddenly he stops in place, turns to her, and there it is. Just so, without his will. Without warning. Caught totally off guard, completely unsuspecting. There's nothing he can do, he can't make out the words Klara is speaking, can't stop them, much less undo the reality behind them. He is absolutely powerless, nobody can help him, nobody can protect him. Not even Neruda. Who knows him like nobody else, knows him and his love for Dora. Not even Dora can help him. His Dora. This cannot be undone.

"I'm pregnant."

Night falls, and it looks like daylight will never come again. Dora.

And everything truly is decided. Now and only now. The finality of the moment.

Chapter 16

Dora hurries home. Every night after every rehearsal she hurries home and sits by the telephone. And waits. And thus the days pass, an infinity of long days without end. Luka had called only once, from the station in Venice, when he'd had to change trains. Since then, nothing. She asks herself if her telephone might be broken—but that surely couldn't be the case, she's checked and made sure—or maybe he's forgotten her telephone number—which she can't imagine—or maybe he's dead—but that's forbidden. What can it mean?!

Dora is not doing well. She can't concentrate on her work, she walks around like a ghost, and asks everyone what could have happened. Helena, Jeanne and even her father try to soothe her: Luka's got a lot to take care of, they say; he's probably working really hard, keeping busy so he can get back to her faster, maybe he called when she wasn't home . . . Because everyone believes that Luka loves Dora and that the two of them belong together. They try to distract her, they're imaginative and resourceful. But it's all for nothing. Only a call from Luka can salvage the situation. "Why don't you call him?" they ask. But Dora has no number, Luka didn't give her one, and she hadn't thought to ask for it, she'd simply forgotten. Things like that happen. It's strange, they think, but they don't say so.

After a week of waiting, Dora is sick from worry, uncertainty and grief. She can't get out of bed, she tells the theater that she's come down with a bad case of flu. Frédéric, the director, who wears flashy pocket squares, calls to wish her a speedy recovery, tells her they're counting on her, she's got to hurry up and get well, they don't have a lot of time, and there are still a few glitches to work out, but she's not to worry, she's just got to take care of herself and get well as soon as possible, and keep rehearsing her lines, opening night is around the corner. Yes, yes, Dora says impatiently and hangs up. Then she dials a short number, for the international operator, and the call goes through. The phone rings a long time, a very long time—probably everyone in the world wants the number for the Hotel Park in Makarska, Yugoslavia, right now. But then she gets the number, after a brief search, and writes it down on a big, blank piece of paper. The telephone number. Dora stares at it. Now what? Dial it, that's always a good start. Soon she gets through. Today's a good day for phone calls.

"Hotel Park, good morning." A high, female voice. She waits, because Dora is unable to speak.

"Hello? Hotel Park, what can I do for you?"

Dora hangs up and starts to cry. There's nothing she can do for Dora, this nice woman with the high voice; she can't give her an explanation, she can't send Luka to her. The worst is, she likely knows something that Dora doesn't know. It's humiliating. At this moment, she hates Luka. She doesn't understand anything.

But she can't help herself, she calls again. She has no choice. Anything else feels like dying.

"Hotel Park, good morning." A high, female voice.

"Good morning, may I please speak to Mr. Ribarević?"

Dora doesn't recognize her own voice. It's as if she were disguising it.

"And who may I say is calling?"

Dora is silent. What can she say?

"Hello? Are you still there?"

"Yes. My name is Negrini."

"Mr. Ribarević is away from the hotel at the moment. He'll be back in the afternoon."

"When is the best time to reach him?"

"Try around three o'clock." The voice is still friendly. And high.

"Thank you."

"You're welcome. Good-bye."

"Good-bye."

Dora hangs up and feels depleted, as if she'd been dragging nets full of fish out of the sea all day. Or as if she'd learned all of Shakespeare's female roles in twenty-four hours. She closes her eyes and waits. She would rather do anything but wait.

A little before two o'clock, Helena comes in and brings her lunch. Dora peevishly sends her away. She wants to be alone when she speaks on the phone with Luka's father. Helena hovers in the kitchen; she's beside herself with worry. Dora hears her call Marc and tell him to come over right away. Dora imagines Marc protesting that he's writing, that he can't leave his work just like that. That he's on an incredible roll, he's written ten pages in two hours. But Helena is crying already, and Marc is surely on his way over. A little before three, he appears in Dora's living room and knocks gently on her bedroom door, sticks his head in, and as soon as Dora sees him, she starts to cry. Helena hurries to her side, tries to hug her and hold her tight, but Dora shouts at her to leave her alone. Helena and Marc leave the bedroom and sit at the table in the kitchen. Dora can see them through the wall: Helena is distraught, Marc wants to go home and go back to writing. But he stays, all the same, drinking red wine he found in the cupboard. "How can you drink now," Dora hears Helena fuss. "This is pure and simple not the time for that, we need to keep clear heads." Marc doesn't respond, but he probably keeps sipping his wine; it gives him the strength to stay with Helena in the kitchen and deal with the situation.

During this whole time, Dora does not once take her eye off the clock. She follows the minute hand as if it were her heartbeat. Three o'clock.

"Hotel Park, good afternoon." A deep masculine voice.

Dora is so startled that she hangs up. And calls right back.

"Hotel Park, good afternoon." A deep masculine voice. This time, gently questioning.

"Hello, may I please speak with Mr. Ribarević?"

Dora's voice trembles.

"This is he. And to whom am I speaking?" Now his voice is openly curious.

"Dora Negrini." So, now it's done. It's out. Now she's going to have to face it. No more uncertainty. Everything will be cleared up, and she will see that she's upset herself for nothing. The worst is behind her. She has to cry again, this time from joy and relief.

"Dora Negrini? Do we know each other?"

And suddenly she falls into a deep pit, she's in endless free fall. This is it.

"Hello, Ms. Negrini, are you still there?" The worried voice of the man who is Luka's father.

Darkness surrounds Dora.

"Hello! Can you hear me?"

Dora stirs, opens her mouth, nothing comes out.

"Ms. Negrini, are you all right?" Concerned, but also a little annoyed.

"It's me, Dora. Dora. I was very little. Back then, in Makarska. And we were always together, inseparable. And then I went away. I didn't want to, but my parents . . . We moved. It's me. Dora." This can't be her, no, not this stammering, nonsense-spouting person.

"Dora? Luka's Dora?"

And the sun shines again, and the world rights itself and takes a bow. A fabulous achievement. A once-in-a-lifetime performance. And curtain.

"Yes."

"Luka's little friend Dora? I can't believe it!"

Something is wrong with these words, and Dora clings to the edge of the precipice. Something is definitely wrong. Her muscles quiver from tension. How long can she endure this?

"May I speak to Luka?" Where does this voice come from?

"Well, yes, Luka isn't here. He's at home."

"Yes. Can I speak to him?"

A silence, tinged with doubt and confusion.

"I can give you his number . . ."

"Yes, I'd like to speak to Luka."

He tells her the telephone number and Dora writes it down.

"Thank you. Good-bye."

She hangs up without giving him the chance to say good-bye.

Then she falls asleep. Her last thought is devoted to the prince, who must awaken her with a kiss. For a change.

In the kitchen, while all of this is going on, and afterward, the wine keeps flowing.

Days have passed. Dora has left her bed, and yesterday, she went back to rehearsals at the theater. Frédéric, sporting red and orange, had hugged her, then taken a leap back and asked if she really was better, it would be a tragedy, more tragic than *King Lear* itself, if he were to come down with anything. Dora had smiled faintly and done her best to reassure him that there was no danger that anyone in the ensemble would fall sick. What she didn't say was that she wasn't sick. Not with anything contagious, at any rate. Then Frédéric had asked her about Luka, and her eyes had widened and filled with tears, and she'd run off and hid in the cloakroom. They had trouble getting her back onto the stage.

Today, though, she got up early. Today is the day. She's decided. She sits on the sofa by the phone and breathes deeply in and out. Just as she'd learned to do, and as she'd taught Luka. In and out. Deep and long. Her left hand is already on the receiver. The right is on her diaphragm, to monitor her breathing. Then the left hand takes the whole phone, lays it in her lap. The left hand brings the receiver to Dora's ear, and the right hand dials the number. Dora breathes calmly. From her diaphragm. In through her nose, and out through her mouth. Three times deeply. And she's calm like the sea at twilight, after a shower of rain.

It rings. It's eight in the morning. It rings three times. Then Luka answers.

"Hello?" There it is, the voice that belongs to her. There he is, her man. Dora can't speak. Everything is forgotten. There's only him, and this love that's bigger than the world.

"Luka, it's Dora." She whispers.

"Dora." His voice like ice cream in the summer sun.

"Luka, my darling, my love! Come back to me." She caresses the mouthpiece with her lips. Her whole body trembles, as if it could feel Luka's touch.

"Dora." And then nothing more. As if ice cream weren't condemned to melt in the summer sun.

"Luka, what's happened? Come back to me. It's been weeks, what are you still doing there? Why haven't you called me? I've almost gone out of my mind, I couldn't even go to the theater. I've stayed in bed, waiting for you, waiting for you to call, where are you? What are you still doing there? Come to me. To us. Like we planned. Luka." And suddenly she's tired, and a kind of apathy envelops her, as if she suspects what is coming next.

"Dora. It's over." Luka's voice is quiet and unrecognizable.

"Papou died."

"I'm sorry." Impatient.

"Luka, my love, I miss you. What would Neruda say? Come, give me just one verse, I long to hear it."

"Dora." Luka groans.

"Breathe, Luka, breathe." She can hear him counting. "Breathe, my prince, breathe."

They are hundreds of miles apart. Their lips cannot touch. All their fingers have are memories. Despair courses through hundreds of miles of cable.

"Dora. Farewell."

"No. Without you? Luka, remember."

Silence.

"*El amor supo entonces que se llamaba amor. / Y cuando levanté mis ojos a tu nombre / tu corazón de pronto dispuso mi camino.*"

A noise, as of someone struggling for air.

"Sonnet seventy-three. I didn't forget. I looked it up. You're right. That's us, Luka!"

"Dora. I have to go. Don't call me again. Ever." Pause. "Please."

And he's gone.

Only the monotonous drone from the receiver.

And he's gone.

Life is gone. The past and the future. No more barefoot walks. No more ice cream. It's too late. Nothing and no one can be kept safe any longer. Their eyes, hundreds of miles from each other, stare silently at nothing for hours, until they begin to ache. Nevertheless they don't move them. They don't want to pretend that they're not afraid, that they're not alone. Abandoned, destroyed. Completely. Everything gone. Never to return. No more secret home. No more shared home together, who could bear it. Nothing is real anymore. From this day forward everything will be forgotten. Must be forgotten. As if it had never happened. Only memories, unwelcome memories. That ache. Over. Everything. No more Luka. And Dora. No more Dora. No more world. No curtain. No bow. No more waiting. No hope. Dead. Forever and ever. Deaddeaddeaddeaddeaddeaddeaddeaddead.

Like Papou, who'd died two days ago. Old and happy. Who'd everything and had to renounce nothing. Dora wishes she were Papou. And Luka, too. Dead. Forever and ever.

Chapter 17

Opening night. Dora does facial exercises. She stands at the window and loosens up her jaw. She makes noises. Nobody bothers her. Everyone's caught up in their own preparations. They're all professionals. Like Dora. The scented April breeze wafts gently across her face. The time has come. This is her life. This is what she's always wanted. A dusty stage, a red curtain and the audience. Her audience. She needs nothing else.

There will be no questions asked. Many glances will be avoided.

"Today's the big day, little one," Frédéric calls out in a stage whisper, and smiles at her. Today he's dressed in chartreuse and black, very elegant, and already he's hurrying up to the others and encouraging them. Running around cackling in excitement like a hen who's laid an egg.

Dora doesn't need that. Doesn't need the egg, doesn't need to be bucked up. She knows what she's capable of and how good she is. She takes one last probing look in the mirror and attentively inspects her face for a few minutes. Everything's as it should be. She's not herself anymore. She's Cordelia. And she's prepared to die.

The show is a great success.

Afterward, Dora is surrounded by her family and friends. Everyone congratulates her and toasts her. She's happy. She's pleased with herself and with her performance. Frédéric praises her and says, his eyes wet with jubilant tears, that she's the theater world's newest star. She's only twenty-two years old. She can already spot a few jealous glances in the crowd, but tonight they don't bother her. The world is hers for the taking. So says Frédéric. Except for . . . Oh, nothing. Let's forget about that.

Back in her apartment, deep in the night of her first big, genuine triumph, as Dora stands alone at the window of her darkened living room, looking out at the lights of the city that is her home, she unexpectedly comes to a decision. This surprises her. It hadn't been clear to her that a decision needed to be made, since everything had been decided already. But all at once, she's rocked by a realization that hits her with the kind of force a person cannot endure and remain standing, like a hurricane wind that knocks you over, and she knows with her whole body and her whole mind, with all of her thoughts and senses and desires, that she cannot imagine never again feeling Luka's body next to hers. The pain is physically unendurable. Like being buried alive. The nightmare of her life. Standing at the window, she realizes that she must be true to herself, that she has no choice but to fight.

As she comes to a decision, she feels the balmy April air fill her lungs. She breathes.

Chapter 18

It's the first time in sixteen years. This gorgeous city on a perfect bay. At the foot of a tall mountain that you can climb, if you feel like it. The sea everywhere. It shimmers silver in the morning sun, like eternity. Like the house of God. Dora is overwhelmed. Her eyes get wet and she hides them behind big black sunglasses.

A beautiful young woman. At the reception desk. In a tight, dark blue dress. Flat white sandals. Two big trunks. A white handbag. Fingers full of rings. Long, curly hair. Unruly. It gets in her eyes. She keeps blowing it away. Blue-white earrings. A narrow face. Full lips. A wide nose. Big, dark eyes. Impatient hands. An elegant watch.
Dora.

"Dora."
Luka is already counting: one, two, three, four . . . and Dora quickly finds the way behind the reception desk, and presses her body against his, lays her mouth on his mouth and whispers softly to him:

"You are my prince, don't fall asleep, you are my prince, only mine, stay with me, look at me, look into my eyes. I'm here, everything's all right, it's over, everything is fine, my prince." Luka sinks into the swivel chair beside him as if he has no muscles. No will. As if he were one of those old, holey air mattresses that are always turning up in unexpected places at the hotel, left behind by their departed owners. Luka's eyes are closed and his breathing is labored. Some things in life a person can't ever be prepared for. He feels Dora's head on his stomach, her arm around his waist, but oxygen is in short supply at the moment, so he keeps sitting there, motionless. He feels the pressure of her body, and it's strange and wonderful at the same time, and he wants to keep her here and push her away at the same time. He opens one eye, he has no strength for anything more, and sees her in front of him, on her knees, her long hair in his lap, and the happiness overwhelms him and crushes him at the same time. He hears her murmur, her voice doesn't quite reach him, but it might be the word "prince" that leaves her mouth. He lays his hand on her hair.

Dora pauses and raises her head, Luka is struck by her glance, unprepared. Her eyes are damp, and her lips move, forming the word that he anticipates, and Dora knows that Luka knows that he has lost. Is lost. Because he has won: She's there, and whatever happened is now over, and now the cards are being reshuffled, and she can tell already that she's holding trumps, she can only win, which means Luka will win, too. Has already won. Because anything can happen in a single second. Everything is to be expected. With every breath, everything can change.

"Let's get out of here."

Chapter 19

A tiny hotel room. Like a whole universe. Like a whole life. Without borders. Endless. Infinite. Like the depths of the ocean. Unexplored. Full of secrets. Frightening. Irresistible. Fascinating. Like the number of stars in the sky. Unknown. Unsettling. Indestructible. Immortal.

They lie in each other's arms on the rumpled bed. She refuses to let the sheets cover her body. He rests his chin on her hair. They don't want to talk yet. Talking will spoil everything, and unleash truths that neither of them wants to hear. No, talking will have to wait. So they make love again. Their bodies next to each other. Sweaty. Tired. Hungry. Insatiable. Happy. On the damp sheets. A hand on the stomach. A fingernail on an upper arm. Mouth on breast. Leg over hip. His green eyes. And then they make love yet another time. So as not to forget what they have together, who they are, where they come from, and to whom they belong. And as they rest, deeply intertwined, looking into each other's eyes, they understand, and know that the other also understands, that love has learned, just in this moment, that it is called love.

"I'm hungry, I haven't eaten anything since yesterday."

"Did you fly?"

"No, I wanted to go the same way you did."

He kisses her.

"When the train stopped in Venice, I even called my number in Paris, like you did."

He smiles and kisses her again.

"Luckily, nobody answered."

He leans his nose against her forehead.

"When I saw the town here, I started to cry."

He gently brushes away her tears, though they'd dried hours before.

"And the sea. I'd almost forgotten it."

"Yes, the sea."

Dora raises her head a little, enough so she can see Luka, and beams at him.

"I'm hungry, I've got to eat something."

"We can call room service, or we can go to the restaurant. Whatever you want." His fingers trace her movements. Like dancers on a stage. Focused, and intent on making no mistakes.

"Will I be staying in this room?"

"I'm not sure, I'll have to double check the reservations."

"But which room had you reserved for me? This one has no sea view."

"I don't understand what you mean."

"I booked a room at this hotel, with sea view, a week ago."

"What? I didn't know anything about it. I was out at sea for two weeks, I took time off; it was wonderful. I went fishing with a friend, Vinko—you've got to meet him. This is my first day back at work, I haven't even looked at the reservations book, I had no idea that you . . . What name did you book the room under? Nobody told me anything. Did you talk to my father? Did he know about it? He didn't tell me anything. Did you come alone? How long are you staying?"

"I'm staying two weeks."

"And I'm married."

Chapter 20

Dora and Luka sit in the empty hotel restaurant, where everything is dark brown—wooden tables and wooden chairs, wooden benches and brown floor tiles. Like bittersweet chocolate. Only the tablecloths are red-and-white-checked. The walls are painted white, and hung with paintings with nautical themes. Almost all of them come from Luka's collection. Dora recognizes them right away without ever having seen them before. They command the room with their color, nothing else in the room has any importance. She recognizes the brushwork. Slanting, and very flat, where he'd borne down on the brush with the pressure of his extended thumb.

Dora and Luka sit in the empty hotel restaurant. Each of them sunk in their own thoughts, like two Spanish caravels laden with gold in the middle of the Atlantic, engulfed by stormy winds and waves. Thoughts that resemble each other like identical twins.

They have already ordered. For Dora, a large order of baked noodles with cheese and a big salad; for Luka, an order of French fries.

They drink wine, they always drink wine when they eat together. The waiter greets Luka warmly and looks at Dora curiously but says nothing. Luka had checked with the front desk and found someone to fill in for him, even though his shift was almost over anyway. He found a room for Dora, a pretty one. With a sea view, naturally. He carried her trunks to her room and arranged everything himself. Luka treats his guests well. And Dora is more than a guest. She is his life.

The food comes quickly, they are the only guests. They eat in silence. There's too much to digest. It's been a remarkable day, full of surprises. Dora is genuinely hungry, her fork travels swiftly, relentlessly, from the plate to her mouth. Luka eats because food is in front of him, but he doesn't have much of an appetite. He's too worked up. He has to concentrate on his breathing; he's got to remember not to close his eyes. Dora's presence makes this easier, because he has to keep on looking at her, to make sure she's really there, across from him. It can't really be her, he thinks, she belongs to another life, to the life that ought to be his, his real life that he can no longer have. Then again, it can only be her, because she is his life, the real one. Dora eats, says nothing and doesn't look at him. After a little while, he starts to feel scared.

Finally, the plates are empty and cleared. At last. The second bottle of wine is ordered. Dingač from the Pelješac peninsula, the best red wine in the country. Luka gives the waiter—who keeps looking at him questioningly and at Dora curiously—the sign that he wants to pour the wine himself. And he does. They take their glasses and raise them, clink them. Their eyes lock.

"So, and now tell me that what you said isn't true, that it was only a tasteless joke. Quickly, tell me quickly." Dora's voice is calm and controlled. Luka recognizes it, it's her professional voice. He's power-less against it. And yet . . . "And don't even think about fainting." He's powerless. To the core. She can see right through him.

"No, unfortunately, I can't tell you that. Though there's nothing I would rather do." Luka's voice is quieter than quiet, neither of them knows where this will take them.

"I don't understand. In February we were still together and in love. Now it's May and you are married. Were you married then?"

"No. I wasn't married then. Then I wanted to marry you. I still do. You are my wife."

"Forever and ever. I know. But it sounds like there's somebody else who would not agree." No irony. No despair. Not yet.

"And yet."

"Make me understand. I need to understand this, or I'm going to fall down and die."

"It's simple and it's not. It's a long story." Luka takes a swig of wine. He suspects that now the part is coming that frightens him the most when he's alone.

"I've got at least two weeks." Dora also takes a swig. The great buildup.

"She's pregnant."

"That was quick. The long story, I mean. But the other part, too." She empties her glass. She closes her eyes and smiles.

"Her name is . . ."

"I don't want to know it!"

"We were together for a long time, a while ago, when I was study-ing in Zagreb. Then we broke up. Last summer I came home to Makarska, and there she was, waiting for me. It was nothing serious. No commitment at all . . ."

"So I see."

"I had other women, too, she didn't say anything about it, even if she knew. I have no idea." Luka can't look at Dora. He's afraid of her gaze. He imagines her getting up and leaving him, and that would be the end of everything.

"Then I had the show in Paris. And there you were. End of story. There is only you. As long as I know you."

"But she's pregnant."

"Yes, by me."

"Are you sure?"

Luka is silent. What can he say?

"How could that have happened?"

"That you know."

"Didn't you use protection?"

"She said she was on the Pill."

"And you?"

"I wasn't on the Pill." That doesn't land well. Not at all. This is no time for jokes. "I used condoms. Most of the time."

Dora pounds her fist on the table.

"How could this have happened?"

"I don't know." Luka really doesn't know. He believes in poetic justice, but he doesn't say that to Dora.

"It's unfair."

"Yes, I guess so."

"What do you mean, you guess so?"

"I've already said, it's complicated."

"What's complicated about it? So far, everything you've told me is very simple and straightforward." Dora leans across the table. Her features are distorted.

"There's a backstory." Luka speaks slowly and softly.

"I understand that, but that's no reason . . ."

"She was . . ."

"What's her name?"

Luka looks at her uncertainly.

"I want to know what her name is."

"But earlier . . ."

"I don't want to deal with phantoms, if I . . ." Dora leans back in her chair again and does breathing exercises. Luka recognizes that. "So, what's her name?" Her voice is calm, which Luka does not find reassuring. On the contrary.

"Klara."

"Klara."

"Yes, Klara."

A loaded silence. As if there were suddenly three of them at the table. As if now everything has been said, and therefore everything is completely clear. Curtain. *Exit Dora.*

"Let's go to the rock."

With each step, everything becomes more familiar, clearer, more beloved. The sea, the pebbles, the yellow house, the narrow path to the lighthouse. As if they'd never changed. As if she had never gone away. Dora feels like crying. And even that is a childhood memory. They stand behind the lighthouse. They look out to sea. Everything imaginable comes to mind. Gulls cry overhead. A gentle breeze rustles Dora's curls.

"Can it really be that I only got here a couple of hours ago?" It's as if she were talking to herself.

"It feels more like you never went away."

Luka takes her in his arms and kisses her. She kisses him back. They linger there a long while.

"Let's go farther out."

And they head toward the rock, warmed by the afternoon sun. They pass two couples on the way, who take no interest in them.

"It must be here somewhere." Dora looks excitedly over a ledge, toward the depths.

"Yes, only a couple more steps, come on."

Luka pulls her along farther, and behind an intoxicatingly fragrant gorse bush he starts the downward climb. He follows the narrow path and Dora follows him. She feels dizzy from the flood of memories that engulf her. They're like shoves in the back, pushing her forward. Only a few steps more, then another few, and they're there, crouching before the hidden opening of the tunnel. They look at each other.

"We're too big!" Dora doesn't want to believe it.

"Nonsense, we'll manage. It just won't be as easy as it was sixteen years ago." Luka laughs confidently.

"Then you go first."

"Happily, my love—you were always a scaredy-cat."

"Me? That can't be true. I'm not . . ."

Luka covers her words with his mouth and kisses her; and she stops talking and squabbling.

"You haven't changed at all. I love you."

"You aren't allowed to say that to me."

"It's the truth."

"Maybe it doesn't matter. Maybe the other truth is more important. Maybe there's a top-ten list of truths, and . . ."

Luka resumes his earlier maneuver, with gratifying results.

"It'll be dark soon, let's crawl through."

And Dora shoves him into the tunnel and follows him. Blindly. Even though she knows that he can't be relied upon unconditionally. But she doesn't care.

With difficulty, but giggling, they reach the end of the tunnel and stand up straight again. Their rock looms in front of them, so full of memories, images, thoughts and hours of silent togetherness that they have to cling to each other to avoid slipping on the damp, salty stone. It's overwhelming. Matchless.

"Let's look at clouds. I bet I'll beat you again!"

Dora and Luka lie on the rock, looking up at the scattering of clouds that play across the sky.

"There! A baby!"

Luka says nothing. He tries to see it, but his vision is blurry.

"I'm sorry, I didn't mean . . ."

"That's all right, forget it."

They fall silent. Dora takes Luka's hand.

"Why did you have to marry her?"

"Because I couldn't do it twice. I just couldn't."

"I don't understand."

"I got her pregnant once before, and I didn't want the baby, and she had an abortion, and I left her. Once should be enough."

Dora sits down and leans over Luka. Tenderly, gently, she runs her hand across his face.

"That's awful. I'm sorry."

"The first time I really was a pig, I treated her so badly. I liked her, but once she told me she was pregnant—and she told me in front of my father and Ana—I panicked. I couldn't breathe, my whole life rebelled against it. It just wasn't right, nothing was right. I didn't even say anything about it to her, directly, but it was obvious how I felt, and she did what I wanted without my having to say it. She suffered so much, and loved me so much, she would have done anything I wanted, but I, I couldn't bear it, and she didn't even fight it, I thought it was so awful, that I just left, I went away without a word to her, nothing, I was cruel. I felt so ashamed, but I couldn't do anything else. It felt like my life was ending."

Dora hugs him. She rocks him back and forth, and knows he hasn't confided this to anyone before.

"There are always two people in a relationship, both of them make mistakes, and both bear responsibility."

"Yes, but sometimes one more than the other."

"You're right. Running away is no solution."

The sun goes down. The air is aromatic and mild and beguiling. Dora feels like she could be six years old again. Time is so treacherous.

"But couldn't you have taken responsibility for the child without marrying her?" Dora whispers. These are the most important moments of her life, and knowing this makes her gentle and thoughtful and tentative, open to anything. But it also makes her feel a little dizzy.

"I don't know, maybe. The way it happened, I felt I had no choice, like I had to make things right. Pay my debt."

"Luka, you only owe a debt to yourself."

"I just had this feeling, you know, that I had to do something, like everyone was expecting it from me; nobody said anything, no—but everyone looked at me . . . It's a small town, Dora, a village, everyone knows everyone else, everyone knows everybody's business . . ."

Dora holds Luka like a newborn child, tenderly and carefully, and hopes he will calm down. And stay with her. Undo everything else. Erase it.

"And she didn't say anything, not a single word, just waited, was just there, and before long we found ourselves at the registry office, and I said yes, and fainted . . ."

Dora doesn't know whether to laugh or cry. Everything seems so grotesque to her. Nightmarish.

". . . and you weren't there, until the very last I kept hoping that you would rescue me, like Indiana Jones, or like a . . ."

"Like a proper prince, you mean."

"Like a proper prince."

"But *you're* the prince. My prince, don't you know that anymore?"

"A proper prince."

It's dark, and the air is fresh and still and the sky is full of stars and a waxing moon. It smells of trees in bloom and the sea at peace. Life celebrates itself. Each year anew.

"Do you love her?"

"I love you, and I want to spend my life with you." Luka speaks like someone who has passed his problems along to somebody else, and doesn't have to worry about anything anymore, because someone else will take care of everything, and he can go back to playing with his friends without a care in the world. To build sand castles, even though Makarska has no sandy beaches. Play water polo. Or soccer. Or paint. Just to be himself.

"What do we do now?" It might be a rhetorical question, or maybe Dora is just asking herself, out loud. The question is in no way directed at Luka. So his answer shocks her all the more.

"We could kill her."

Chapter 21

Luka leaves Dora's room. "That was a joke, what you said earlier, right?" she says uncertainly at the door. He looks at her, tired and full of love, and presses against her. "Of course," he whispers. He leaves the hotel. It's three in the morning. They hardly slept a minute. The clear night embraces him, cool and refreshing. Springtime by the sea. Luka is in no hurry to get home. He knows what he should do. He just doesn't know whether he has the courage. He takes a detour. The town suddenly feels too small for him. If only he'd stayed with Dora. With her he feels strong and decisive. But eventually his house rises up in front of him. Ana and Toni are sitting on the steps. Ana just turned twenty-one. When she spots him, she jumps up and runs toward him. Toni stays seated.

"Where were you? We've been looking for you all night! Where were you hiding?" She's only a step away from hysteria, which is unusual for her. Loud and excited, yes; hysterical, no.

"What's wrong? Did something happen?"

Luka feels pleasantly tired, he misses Dora already and doesn't feel like arguing. More than anything, he wants to avoid a fight, and, if possible, to keep out of Klara's way. He doesn't want to get all stirred up, he wants to prolong the feeling of being with Dora.

"What's wrong? Dad took Klara to the hospital hours ago, while you were God knows where!" Ana is really furious, to the point that Toni finally stands up, comes to them and lays a protective arm on Ana.

"Why?"

"Why? Why? Because she's having your baby, you . . . you . . ." She can find no term of abuse to adequately describe how she feels about her brother at this moment.

"But it's still too early." Luka doesn't let himself get sucked into the panic that Ana emotes. Today his life found meaning again. And he doesn't want to jeopardize that.

"Of course it's too early, but she went into labor, and there was nothing to be done, you can't say, Dear baby, it's too early, wait a few weeks more, stay where you are. This won't do, you moron, when the labor pains start, then out comes the baby, and you weren't here, Dad took her to the hospital, and you weren't here, it's your baby, and your wife, where were you, where were you all day, nobody saw you . . ."

"I was busy."

"Busy? What does that mean? Doing what?"

"I had company."

"What kind of company? Dad said you got someone to fill in for you at the hotel. What's the matter with you?"

Luka knows that now is not the time to bring Dora into the conversation. Klara is in the hospital, she's having the baby. She's counting on him. He'd made a promise to her. He'd married her, he'd wanted to take care of her and the baby, that was the commitment he made. At the time, it had seemed like the only right thing to do. Back in her hotel room, in the room Luka had picked out for her, Dora sleeps, trusting him, believing in him and in what they have, what only they have, what only they could have, matchless and unique. Their love, like the boundless ocean.

Luka has to count: one, two, three, four, and to hold his breath, and Ana gives him a smack on the head.

"No bullshit from you, do you hear me?"

Luka looks at her, dumbstruck.

"Get a move on, we've got to get to the hospital!"

Luka's glance wavers between Ana's and Toni's eyes, back and forth, looking for answers. He shakes his head. This can't be. This is wrong. And he gets angry at Klara, who's having the baby too early, and putting him in such an impossible position. Especially today. Little by little, Luka grows furious, profoundly furious, at everyone and everything. Thoughts of hatred, helplessness, grief and bitterness wash over him like a waterfall, and he lies on the ground, gripped with fear.

"What should I do!" The quiet cry of an agonized soul.

Ana looks at him closely, then gives him a quick smile and takes his hand.

"Come on, I'm with you."

And the three of them head off together. And Luka feels like crying.

Dora doesn't have to fall asleep. Because she's already dreaming. With eyes wide open. Nothing can take away this feeling of tranquillity and confidence. And the smile. To sleep would be a waste of time. Life is full of wonder. Dora sits on a chair on her balcony and drinks in the silver shimmer of the sea. She thinks of the moments that determine a life. The moments that can't be anticipated. That are simply, suddenly there. Forever and ever.

In the hospital it's quiet. The place looks abandoned. Like after some natural catastrophe that had no survivors. Toni goes looking for a nurse. Ana holds Luka tightly by the hand and leads him to a row of seats. Orange plastic chairs. Luka looks around. It's the new hospital. Not the one where he and Dora spent hours pretending to be patients, with no appointments and no symptoms. He longs for a time machine.

"Ana, Luka!" Toni calls out softly, making wild gestures. They stand up and follow him. A few corridors on, they stop at a room, and Toni indicates the door with his head.

"Klara is in the delivery room, but Zoran is in here."

They go in. Zoran is lying on a hospital bed, sleeping. Luka smiles. Ana looks at him and smiles, too. It's a time for tenderness. There's only one chair in the room, and Ana takes it. Toni takes his place behind her. Luka leans against the windowsill. He can't see the sea from it. Or the hotel. Unable to see anything that matters to him through the window, he gets scared again. Restlessly, he bumps against the bed. Zoran opens his eyes. No one says anything. There's a long pause, while the father looks at his son, as if he were a puzzle that has to be solved before the stroke of midnight. Or else the coach will turn back into a pumpkin. But it's already nearly four A.M. It's almost light in the east, behind the high mountain peaks that shield the sun like a folding screen. Time's up. Nothing more can be changed. No puzzles can be solved. They will remain mysterious.

"It's taking a long time," says Toni, who's uncomfortable with long silences.

"Yes." Zoran, on the other hand, thinks the less said, the better.

"It's been hours, hasn't it?"

"Yes."

"What did the doctor say?" Finally, Ana comes to her boyfriend's rescue.

"I don't know. At first there was no doctor, then a midwife came, she just looked at her, didn't examine her, and then they came and took her away."

"That was all?"

"Yes."

"Nobody said anything?"

"No."

"Didn't you ask?" Ana is mystified by her father.

"I fell asleep."

"Should I go and try to get news?" Ana asks Luka, who's still looking out the window, searching for his life. He says nothing. This has nothing to do with him, he thinks. Even if he made a promise to Klara and is responsible for her. Every now and then, you take a step back and get an objective look at your life, and marvel at how everything took shape, and see the mistakes you made. Yes, you can do that. It's good to get distance, it's highly recommended, even. But to leave the scene entirely—that's a dangerous thing, not advisable.

"Luka!"

Luka glances at Ana from afar, and says nothing.

"Yes, go, my child." Zoran always wants to keep the peace.

Ana gets up and slowly leaves the room.

"Dawn will break soon."

"Yes," says Luka, and keeps searching.

. . .

Dora jolts awake with a pressure on her breast, she can hardly breathe and her heart beats wildly. Her head is full of images of dead people she doesn't know, who menace her, forming an ever-tightening circle around her, until she can't move. She opens her eyes and lets out a faint cry. She's alone. The bed is cold and she's shaking. She draws the covers up to her chin, and turns onto her other side, so she can see the sea through her open balcony door. Dreamlike. She calms herself and falls back to sleep. Hoping for better dreams.

"It's a girl."

Ana cries and laughs, and hugs Luka and Toni and their father, then Luka again, and hops around in the little hospital room and claps and does pirouettes and can't be stopped. Zoran's eyes fill, and he says over and over, "A girl, a girl," and his smile is full of memories, and he gives Luka a mighty thump on the shoulder, and smiles again, "a girl." Toni, also grinning, thumps Luka on the other shoulder, and doesn't even try to calm Ana down.

"A girl," Luka whispers, and leaves the room. Slowly, but surely. As if he'd found what he was looking for. With the first rays of the sun.

Chapter 22

"Whatare you doing here? Aren't you off until this afternoon?"

Luka walks past the reception desk and says nothing, waves briefly, but doesn't smile. Strange, his friend on the morning shift thinks, and turns his attention back to the guest list.

Luka knocks on the door of Dora's room, and it opens at almost exactly the same moment, as if she'd been waiting for him. Which she had. They hug. They kiss.

"It's a girl."

And now he can smile. He looks into her eyes, and they both start crying, aware that anything is better than being apart.

After they make love, they lie quietly in bed. Now things will be brought up and discussed. Explained and resolved. Grappled with. Not left hanging.

"How are they doing?"

"I don't know."

"What do you mean, you don't know?"

"I left immediately."

Dora has to think about what this means. If anything.

"But it's your daughter. And your wife."

"I know. I know. I've never been more aware of that than I am now. Believe me. Nobody is going to let me forget it."

"The baby's come earlier than expected, I take it?"

"Yes."

Both of them ponder.

"Do you think it might have something to do with us?"

"In what way?"

"Could it be a sign?"

"What kind of sign? Meaning what?"

"I have no idea. I was just wondering."

They try to understand.

"Does she know . . ."

"What?"

"That I exist?" How humble she's become! As if she were entirely inconsequential. Devoid of meaning.

"No." He's sure of this. "At least not from me."

"Who else could have told her? Who did you tell about Paris?"

"Nobody. I didn't have time. I didn't have a chance. Everything happened so quickly . . ."

"Didn't she ask any questions?"

"No."

"She didn't ask why you'd stayed such a long time in Paris?"

"No."

"What kind of woman is that?"

Dora is getting angry. She doesn't like being ignored. It's not for nothing that she became an actress.

"It had nothing to do with her. She knew that."

They fall silent. They don't know where to go next.

It's a beautiful morning.

"I'm hungry."

The breakfast room is empty. The buffet has already been cleared. Luka goes to the kitchen to order breakfast. The cook knows him. The waitress knows him. Everyone in this hotel knows him: He's not only the boss's son, he's also a famous artist, and the people of the coast, like elephants, never forget anything. They all look at Dora curiously, appraisingly.

They sit on the terrace by the sea. It's peaceful. In May there are no children rampaging in the pool yet. Just elderly people who've come to the sunny south to bask in the warmth. Who spend the whole day strolling, hiking or sitting by the sea, and count themselves lucky. Particularly when they write postcards to their friends back home.

They eat in silence. Luka isn't hungry, but eats all the same, to keep Dora company. Their eyes meet constantly. Again and again they touch each other; they can't help it.

They don't see the staff exchanging knowing glances. And everything is obvious. Lovers' faces can't keep secrets. They're an open book. Already they're being talked about. Whispered about. Theories will circulate that explain nothing.

As soon as their plates are empty, they get up. Luka takes Dora's hand.

"Let's get out of here."

. . .

Down on the rock, the only sound is the murmur of the sea.

Dora and Luka lie on the sun-warmed stone, letting their legs dangle in the water.

"I've got a hundred questions. At least."

"Go ahead."

"But first, I want to hear you recite Neruda."

Luka remains mute.

"Or have you forgotten him?"

"Perhaps to be without you, is not to be," he quickly retorts. Luka doesn't look at Dora. He watches the seagulls soaring in the endless heights of the sky. "At night, when everyone's asleep or in their rooms, or when I'm alone in the hotel, I take him out of the drawer and read him aloud, and pretend you're there with me, listening. I get so worked up that I start thinking I'm going to pass out. Without you, there's nothing. Being without you is like not existing. No question about it."

Dora also watches the seagulls coasting in the endless heights of the sky. She's so upset that she feels like she could faint. Actually, that's not quite true. But even that is something she'd like to share with Luka. Like everything else.

"What are you doing at the hotel? How long have you been working there? You never mentioned that." Dora's head rests on his stomach.

"Ever since I found out I was going to be a father."

"What about your painting? Do you still have time for it?"

"I haven't painted at all since Paris. I haven't even unpacked my supplies." Luka's hand rests on Dora's stomach. When he feels the warmth of her body, everything seems different. Possible. Promising.

161

As if soon he'd be able to go out and play with his friends again, without a care in the world. To build those nonexistent sand castles.

"But that's a crime! You're a painter! An artist." She could almost cry, she finds it so immeasurably sad. To have renounced his fundamental self? Then what? What would be left?

"I know. But that doesn't matter. I've got a family to support now."

"That's . . . that's . . ." Some things can't be put into words.

Dora gets up and walks around on the rock. Luka watches her, worried. She fixes her eyes on the stone surface, as if she were searching for dead crabs.

"You cannot do that, you have to paint, you absolutely have to paint. Please!" She comes to a stop in front of him.

"Don't cry, please don't cry."

"I'm not crying."

"You are, too, your eyes are red and wet, they're glittering."

"You know I never cry!"

Dora is furious, she gets louder and more hysterical, and Luka has to stand and put his arms around her, to whisper fondly into her tousled hair and reassure her.

"I will paint again."

"Promise?"

"Promise."

"Cross your heart and hope to die?"

"Exactly." He laughs loudly, and raises her face so he can look into her eyes. "Now that you're here."

"You should go home now. You should go to the hospital and see your daughter." Her eyes are reddening again and growing wet, and her voice quavers, and Luka has to hold her tight again. "You must go see your daughter."

"I'll do it."

"Your daughter."

"Dora."

"It's hard for me to conceive that your daughter is not also my daughter."

They hear the town clock strike noon. Such a ceremonious sound. As if it is heralding some important event.

Chapter 23

Luka comes home. In an hour he has to be back at the hotel, this time to work. But Dora will be there. So much for work! Life is better than *Déjeuner sur l'Herbe*, it's a combination of *Red Buoy* and *Luxe, Calme et Volupté*. The very thought of painting again fills his head with pictures.

Zoran is sleeping in the living room on the sofa. Luka realizes he hasn't slept in more than thirty hours. Maybe that's why he feels like he's drunk. Or maybe it's because Dora's there. Or because he's just had a daughter. Or because his life has turned upside down and everything is threatening to topple and fall into the sea. It can't be stopped. He steps into the shower. The spray of hot water falls on his skin like balm. He closes his eyes, and his head spins with clamorous thoughts and feelings. Twenty minutes later, the water has gone cold, and he turns off the tap and dries off. He leaves his hair damp and uncombed. He gets dressed and quietly leaves the house. Zoran is still asleep. Zoran is not a young man anymore, Luka thinks, and the thought pains him.

It's a long way to the hospital. Fifteen minutes by foot. He walks quickly. He doesn't have much time. At two he has to be back at the hotel. He tries not to think of Klara, and of what he's going to say to her. Or what she's going to say to him. What she's going to expect of him. This thought overwhelms him, and he comes to a stop in the middle of Kačić Square, wants to run away, but he forces himself to keep going. In the hospital, it's comfortably cool. With an unexpected decisiveness, he marches to the room where he learned that he'd become a father the previous night. He doesn't knock, he walks in as if he were at home.

And there she is. Klara. She's sleeping, and Luka's grateful to her for that. Next to her bed stands a second bed, a small one, more like a little glass trunk than a bed, and inside it, something moves. Luka sees unimaginably slender arms, tiny hands and feet, moving aimlessly, jerkily. He tiptoes nearer, he absolutely does not want to wake Klara.

And there she is. His daughter. He looks at her. He wants to see everything at once, even though there's hardly anything to see. He inspects her face. Everything is round, soft and expressionless. Her mouth moves, her eyelids flutter, and that's about it. This is the creature that has thrown his life into utter turmoil. Who has taken painting and Dora away from him. He cannot hate her. But he can't love her either. Looking at her, he tries to imagine that she's his and Dora's daughter. He tries to imagine that he'd wanted her all along, that he'd been happy about her impending arrival, and awaited her birth with longing. He imagines that he and Dora are married, and it was she who had brought this child into the world, and it is she sleeping in that bed . . .

"She's beautiful, isn't she?"

Startled, he takes a step back, as if he'd been caught doing something forbidden.

"I'm so happy." Klara speaks softly, and Luka can't bring himself to look at her. He's miserable. Feelings of guilt surge and swell within him, along with pangs of conscience that he can't drown out.

"How are you?" she asks. As if he were the one who had spent hours in the delivery room, giving birth to their daughter. The obvious injustice of it makes him squirm.

"How are you? Was it rough?" He doesn't recognize his own voice.

"It's over and we're fine. Aren't we?"

Luka looks at her. Her eyes are full of questions she won't ask, for fear she won't like the answers. She gives him her hand. He hesitates only a tiny moment, but she notices, and her smile vanishes. Her glance darkens. She puts her hand on the baby's head.

"You'd rather have had a son, right?"

As it dawns on him that Klara understands nothing, suspects nothing, he realizes there's no need for all his dissembling. So he tells her everything, admits everything, confesses all; though his conscience is clear, he begs her forgiveness, makes promises once again, even cries a little, and reveals his feelings and his thoughts, explaining that he absolutely has to start painting again, because that's who he is, he can't work at the reception desk of a hotel, he's an artist, and if he's to be a painter, his fingers have to be smeared with paint; he speaks without pause and with passion, and before long, all his feelings of guilt evaporate, and he opens up to Klara in full, something he's never done in all the years of their acquaintance and in all the time they've spent together, and he's relieved, he . . .

Luka looks at Klara silently, abstractedly. He casts a brief, despondent glance at the baby in its little bed. His mouth hasn't moved. Not one sound has left his throat. He moans inwardly, consumed by self-loathing.

"I've got to go."

And he's gone. Fled. More coward than prince.

Chapter 24

"A giant, holding a pipe in one hand and a huge ice cream cone in the other."

"You have the imagination of a five-year-old." Luka laughs, a wave of tenderness washes over him.

"What a dumb thing to say! Imagination has no age."

And she's standing up already, and her voice falters, and the boat rocks, and she has to scramble to keep from losing her balance and falling into the sea. Though it wouldn't matter, it's the end of June. But it's only seven-thirty in the morning. She still has her dress on. They haven't even had breakfast yet.

Luka stands up and watches Dora for a moment: Her hands are on her hips, bunched into fists. Spoiling for a fight. Then he tackles her and they both tumble into the sea. With a shriek. Which only disturbs the fish and the seagulls. Because, as far as the eye can see, the two of them are the only human beings between Brač, Hvar and the coast. They laugh and squeal and gulp salty water as if it were the choicest wine, of unknown vintage, the label has been lost. They cavort, splash and dive, and end up in each other's arms, joined at the lips.

"You got my beautiful dress all wet."

"Then, take it off."

"I can't, it's sticking to me."

"I'll help you, then, come on."

And then there's more rollicking and thrashing and shrieking and dunking, and they spit out the sea water, and rub the salt from their eyes.

And then they lie on the deck and make love in the warmth of the early morning sun.

"There! A cradle with a teddy bear sitting in it."

"Right. And can you also see the cigarette sticking out between his sharp claws? And the empty beer bottle beside him?"

Dora looks at him warily. Luka is painting. For several weeks he's been painting again. And yesterday Dora had given him the paints that she'd ordered for him in Paris, with Christian's help. Today he's putting them to use. It's a wonderful sight.

"If you want to be left alone to paint, just tell me, you shouldn't tease me."

"I never tease you, I only please you."

"You men are all the same."

"I love you."

Then a long silence, as they kiss.

"Do you miss Paris?" Luka asks later, as he paints. He's brought several small canvases along. So he can paint small studies of the water. He never gets tired of this. He always discovers something new, a hidden nuance, an unfamiliar movement, a shimmer that arises and blooms only in certain conditions.

"Yes. Most of all I miss the theater."

"Is it going to be a problem for you?" Energetically mixed paint spatters.

"No. I don't know. I don't think so. I'm just taking a couple of months off."

"Do you really want to do that?"

"No. But I want to be with you."

"Then it's not bad at all that good old King Lear broke his leg."

They laugh.

"Yes, that helps a little."

And then they fall silent again, because there's so much left to say and to ask and to decide and to do. Above all, to do. And though the knowledge of this burns in both of them, sometimes keeping them from sleeping, or breathing, they try to avoid thinking about it as often as possible, which isn't all that often, because they live in the thick of these questions, uncertainties and fears. And people. But today, today is a day just for the two of them, a day for them to be alone as a couple, an ideal day to forget about everything, to repress, to defer. Yet perhaps because of this, they don't. Because the day is perfect. The sea. The sun. The air. The sky. The views. It's the way things ought to be. The way their life ought to be. And so they talk.

"I still haven't told Klara anything."

"I know."

"I can't."

"Why not?"

"Whenever I see her, she's got the baby with her."

"Why do you always say 'the baby,' why don't you call her by her name?"

"I don't know. I don't want to get used to her."

"That's ridiculous, my love! She's your daughter, you have to get used to her."

"I don't know. I guess I'm afraid."

Dora hugs him. He likes to lean his head on her shoulder. She smells of salt and sun and of him and of Dora.

"You can love her and be there for her *and* leave her mother. But you can't leave *her,* that you can't do. Absolutely not."

"It's so hard. When I'm with you, everything seems clear. But when I go home and you're not there, I get mixed up and can't figure out what I'm supposed to do, except be with you."

Luka's head slides slowly into Dora's lap.

"You've got to take control of the situation. I can't do it for you. Klara's not my wife, I'm not the one who married her even though I loved somebody else."

Annoyed, Dora pushes his head away. She grows impatient and increasingly anxious.

"Soon it will be two months that I've been here."

"I know, we should celebrate!"

"Luka, I can't take this much longer. The way things are."

He watches as she stands up and stretches then lets her head droop. And he knows he ought to say something, or, even better, do something, the right thing, and he wants to, more than anything in the world he wants Dora, and only her, but it's as if he were sick, or paralyzed. Like he's buried alive in a narrow coffin. And soon he starts to count: one, two, three, four, five . . . His eyes grow heavy and fall closed, he's feeling better now, floating above himself and all his problems . . .

"Stop it! You are mine, only mine, open your eyes, look at me, my prince, I will save you, I will protect you from fire-breathing dragons and wicked witches and enchanted forests, my prince . . ."

Dora kisses his contented face. And they make love.

Once again, nothing is resolved.

Chapter 25

It's been almost two months since Dora returned to Makarska for the first time in sixteen years, and since Luka became a father, after making love to Dora for an entire day and almost an entire night. It's been almost two months since Dora and Luka became inseparable again, like they were when they were young. Nobody in Makarska acts surprised. Nobody asks questions. Not even the people who judge them, who think they're behaving badly. But everyone talks. Everyone looks on with interest, because the town has never seen anything like this before. But nobody laughs either. Because there is still something strange in the air when Dora and Luka are together. You can't call it calm, and you can't call it storm. It smells of mandarin oranges and roasted almonds, of the sea and fresh-baked cookies, and springtime. As if they were enveloped in a cloud. Some people say the cloud is turquoise, others that it's orange. Domica, the ancient, ageless woman who still sits in front of her house on the edge of the woods between the Riva and the beach, says the cloud is light blue, nearly as pale as the sky in summer. Then she nods knowingly and closes her blind eyes. Ever since Domica predicted the earthquake twenty-three years ago, the townspeople have been a little fearful of her. For some of them, that fear amounts to awe; but they still come to her for advice. Especially young women in love. Domica hopes that Dora will come visit her soon, too. She claims to know exactly what Dora needs to do. Some people swear they've seen a little bag with Dora's name on it in Domica's herb cupboard.

Dora has long since moved out of the hotel. It was getting expensive, and she's not famous enough yet. Soon after arriving in Makarska, she visited her aunt Marija, who's still baking those delectable chocolate cakes and was delighted to see Dora again. Over the years, Marija has barely kept in touch with her cousin Helena, so she knows nothing about what Dora's been up to either, about her successes, or about her parents' divorce, and absolutely nothing about Helena's new life. Dora doesn't spend a lot of time at Marija's house, in the small room that her aunt kindly offered her, but Marija is easily satisfied, it's better than nothing, she says, smiling, and when Dora goes out at night and doesn't come back until morning, she doesn't scold her, she just whips up a dream cake to tempt her home and to keep her there. Aunt Marija hears what people say, but she doesn't get involved. She sees how happy Dora is, and how Luka's eyes and whole face light up when he comes to pick her up at the house. She can't blame them, because she remembers how it used to be long ago, when they were children, Dora and Luka, and everything makes sense to her, and she tells people only: "Remember how it was back then!" And they do remember, like real elephants, but worry lines furrow their faces, because they don't know how it all should end, and what's even worse, they don't know anymore what to think, who's the good guy and who's the bad guy. The people of Makarska are extraordinarily caught up in the dilemma, the town has never known anything like it.

These people don't bother Dora, she's glad to have her aunt's support, that's enough for her. Besides, plenty of people are nice to her. She had no trouble getting work at a travel agency: She found a job guiding French-speaking tourists around town, but there are not a lot of them, so she has lots of free time; then again, when any tourists do appear, they're generous with tips, especially once they realize that Dora's an actress, and has come to Makarska for an affair of the heart, so she has enough money. Not that she needs much, anyway. Luka and Aunt Marija's chocolate cake are enough for her, anyway. What could be better for body and soul?

When she comes home on the night of her trip with Luka, happy and a little rumpled, a young woman is waiting for her outside the front door. Dora's first thought is: Klara. But this woman, a girl, really, with light blond hair, seems familiar, she reminds Dora of someone, of something that happened an incredibly long time ago, in another life, she feels a rush of warmth, and smiles, even though the visitor's expression is grave, and remains so.

"You are Dora." It's not a question. She doesn't wait for the answer. "I'm Ana. Luka's sister."

"Ana." Of course! That makes sense! Dora's first live audience. "Ana. How great."

"I'm not so sure of that." Ana says this very slowly, as if she were weighing each word after dredging it up from some hidden crevice of her brain. As if, since last they met, she'd been living on a desert island, and lost the habit of speech.

Dora extends her hand to Ana, but doesn't touch her. She reads something in Ana's face, a deep disquiet, a firm resolve, but also a kind of suppressed longing. Dora does nothing. She waits. Ana remains silent. Dora doesn't invite her into the house. She simply waits for another word from Ana. It's good to wait when a situation is unclear.

Minutes pass. They look at each other.

"I need to talk to you."

"Gladly."

"I want you to go away again. Back where you came from."

Dora says nothing, waits. But she's a little bit taken aback.

"Luka has a family. A daughter. He doesn't need you at all. Leave him alone. He could be happy with the two of them, but first you have to leave him alone."

Dora absorbs what Ana has said, and doesn't contradict her. With each word that Ana speaks, her words come more and more fluently, as if she's finally found the hiding place where they all were stored, and she becomes more and more upset.

"He likes Klara, they've been together such a long time, they've known each other for ages, they've shared a lot, they've been through a lot together. Klara already lost a baby of his, they have a history. She's always been there for him, she never left him, she never moved away, she never forgot about him, she kept track of him, never was ashamed to, she's reliable. Whereas you—you're just going to disappear again, without a word, you're going to leave him and hurt him again, and I'll be the one left picking up the pieces and looking after him and his family, and you won't give it a second thought, you'll just be gone, becoming an actress; I've heard you actually did become an actress, congratulations, so you've got what you always wanted, your photographs in the magazines, so what are you looking for here, nobody wants you . . ."

Dora takes a step toward Ana, wants to fold her in her arms, because at this moment, Ana seems to be three or four years old at most. Dora understands her, and feels how hard it must have been on her when everyone left—her father, her mother, her brother, and Dora had gone, too, she was the first to leave. She wants to hug Ana and apologize, but Ana shocks Dora and herself by slapping her in the face.

Dora touches her cheek, and Ana stares at her.

"I'm sorry. Please excuse me." And then Ana runs away, like a cat from a bad dog.

Dora wants to run after her, but a small group of tourists from Belgium is waiting for her to take them on a dinner tour of Makarska's restaurants.

Rubbing her stinging cheek, she enters the house. Aunt Marija stands at the top of the stairs, shaking her head. "My Dorrie, dear child," she says plaintively. "What will come of this?" her anxious eyes ask. "Where will this whole thing lead?" Marija doesn't have much instinct for such things; she's never been in love, she never got married, she just looked after her parents and baked and thought that was enough. The only uncertainty life has ever thrown her way was whether or not a particular batch of dough would rise. That's how simple life should be, she thinks. And now this. Dora. Her little Dora.

At midnight Dora bids good-bye to her tour group with many hugs and kisses in front of the Hotel Meteor, the newest and biggest hotel in the town, and slowly walks in the direction of Hotel Park. Luka is on the night shift. She takes the beach promenade along the Donja Luka Bay. She doesn't hurry. She chooses her steps carefully, as if she'd had too much to drink, which of course she hasn't. She stares at her toes, emerging from her sandals, and walks, deep in thought. She's startled when another pair of women's feet enters her field of vision. Ana.

Ana looks tired. As if she'd been asleep, but had been shaken awake and brought to the promenade by force.

"I need to talk to you."

"Is that a euphemism for a slap in the face?"

"I'm sorry. Really."

Dora doesn't say a word. She's still thinking. And it's getting late. And Luka's waiting for her. Though this conversation is overdue and could be interesting.

"I don't know why I did it."

"Possibly because you were enraged."

"Maybe, but I had no right. Really."

Dora doesn't say what she's thinking, or what she thinks made Ana so angry. It's late and Luka is waiting for her.

"I don't remember you well. But the impression stuck with me. And the taboo that surrounded your name." Ana smiles awkwardly. Dora smiles, too. She understands. She'd had her own taboos. For sixteen years.

"And now what?"

"The question is, what are your intentions?" Ana looks at Dora, tired and expectant.

"I don't know. I love Luka. And he loves me."

"But he's married. And he has a baby."

"He married the wrong woman, for the wrong reasons. He loves me. I am his life. Nothing else matters." Dora is tired, too, and doesn't like having to explain things that concern only her and Luka.

"That's a very self-serving and irresponsible attitude."

"Do you want him to spend his whole life with a woman he doesn't love, when he knows that I'm in the world? Do you want that for your brother?" Dora feels tears coming. She steps aside, wanting to leave. Ana grabs Dora's arm and Dora stops.

"I want him to be happy, but he has responsibilities all the same. A person can't just think of himself."

Dora looks at her a long time without saying anything. There's nothing to say. Ana has the right to think what she wants. Dora doesn't have to convince her, that's not her job.

"I want to go now." Dora's voice is small.

"To Luka?"

"Yes." And Dora shakes off Ana's hand and walks away, slowly and hesitantly. As she reaches the end of the stone steps, she hears Ana say "I hate you," and the words hit her hard. Her whole body stings, like when you dive wrong off the high board. She runs up the stairs and stands breathless in front of the glass-walled entry to the hotel. She can see Luka standing at reception, talking with the bartender, Jozo, who's obviously about to head home. They laugh loudly and Jozo slaps his thigh. Luka's eyes shine as green as, as . . . oh, Dora has no idea like what, no comparison comes to mind, but they belong to her, those eyes. And that's all that counts.

She walks into the lobby. Luka sees her and stops laughing. He opens his arms. Dora has come home.

Chapter 26

Luka stands in front of the open refrigerator, trying to cool his body and to catch a draft of fresh, breathable air. It's not even six A.M. It's going to be an extremely hot day.

Everything is quiet in the house, though he doubts anyone is sleeping, not in this heat. He takes out a carton of milk and closes the refrigerator door. He's about to sit down at the table when he sees Klara in the kitchen doorway. She's been standing there watching him for who knows how long. Luka tries to smile, but it doesn't feel natural; it feels strained. He says, "Good morning." But Klara just keeps staring at him. Luka decides against sitting down at the table, suddenly he's in a hurry, and he drinks the milk from the carton. Standing. It does him good. Cools him from the inside. Then he takes a first step toward the door.

"Luka, sit down."

Klara's voice is completely awake, as if she'd hardly slept. Luka wouldn't know. He's been sleeping on the living room couch for months, ever since Klara and the baby came home.

"I've got to go now, I've got to be at the hotel at six."

"Sit down, this is important."

And Luka once again feels the unbearable heat, and starts sweating, and knows he'll have to change his shirt.

"Does it absolutely have to be now?"

"As if you would have the time later, or ever!"

Luka doesn't answer. She's right. He'd never have the time. That's how it's been these last months, always on the run. Maybe it really is time to call a halt to it all, to bring everything into the open.

"Fine." He sits at the kitchen table. "Here I am."

Klara draws nearer and sits across from him. Luka hasn't seen her face this close up for a long time. She's tired and exhausted and unhappy, and there's not much life in her eyes. The sight pains him. He can't take much more of this.

"What's going on?" Klara's voice trembles a little.

"What do you mean?" Luka knows how stupid and hurtful his question is, it's offensive, really, but he's playing for time as he gathers his strength.

"People are talking, Luka. In this town, you can't keep a secret for long."

"I know." He inhales deeply and exhales loudly. Klara begins to cry noiselessly, and for Luka that's the signal. It's now or never. "I love her, she means everything to me. I've known her my whole life. We were separated for sixteen years, and then we met again by accident in Paris, and that's it. I love her." And suddenly he can breathe more easily, his lungs are full of oxygen, he feels like he has wings. The nightmare is over. At last. He's done it. He's free. He's said it. No going back. He can't help smiling, and he feels his face light up. Full of pride. "I love her."

"And what about me? And what about Katja?" Klara talks and cries. She's almost whispering.

"Klara, you know why we got married. You know it was only because of the baby, and that otherwise . . ."

It isn't easy for Luka to say this. He's got nothing against Klara, and he knows that everything is basically his fault. He'd let himself get involved with her again, even though he hadn't wanted to. She was always there, waiting, that's true, but he'd had a choice, nobody had forced him. He hadn't thought about anything. She was just there, docile, willing to accept whatever he might offer, never questioning him, never saying anything, never complaining. She was just there. Damn it! He'd never felt strongly about Klara, she could have been anyone. But now they are married, and he's found Dora again. And there's a child now, too, his child. His daughter. Katja. Yes, her name is Katja.

And suddenly he has to get up, hurries out of the kitchen and almost runs into the big bedroom where the crib is, where his daughter sleeps despite the heat, her mouth open. Katja. Her fists spar and jerk, as if she were boxing with a ghost. Katja. His daughter. He leans over the bed and carefully lays his index finger against her rosy cheek. She seems to register the contact for a second, but keeps sleeping fitfully.

Luka feels a hand on his back. Klara stands behind him.

"Take a look at her, our daughter. Your daughter. Isn't she worth it, doesn't she deserve a proper family?"

This isn't a question that can be answered, or should be. Luka contemplates the tiny face. Nothing here is proper. Least of all the family that Klara talks about.

"Can you imagine not seeing her, not spending every day with her, not holding her . . ."

Luka's back stiffens. He's covered in sweat. He senses what has just happened before he fully understands it. Even though he's never held Katja once. He's spent no time with her. He's been a terrible father. At this moment, he begins to hate Klara. From this moment on, it's her fault.

Without a word, Luka leaves the room and the house. His life. Without changing his shirt.

Chapter 27

The August sun burns the skin, even in the shade. Dora drinks a second glass of water. Greedily. As if there weren't enough to go around. She's wearing a white flowing dress. And sunglasses and a straw hat. She's fully accessorized. Zoran sits across from her. His sunglasses are on the table, next to his beer glass. They look at each other. It won't be an easy discussion. It's about the person that both of them love more than anyone else.

"So, what did you want to tell me?" Dora doesn't feel as confident as she sounds, but it's worth keeping in mind that disguising herself is her job.

"I remember when you were still a very little girl. How you went around everywhere with Luka, how the two of you went out on the boat. You were inseparable." He sinks into a reverie of fatherly nostalgia. His glance is opaque. Dora can't read much into it beyond the memory of a little boy and his still littler playmate.

"Did you want to discuss that with me?" The sentence must be spoken.

"No, of course not." Zoran registers her presence again. He smiles warmly and fondly. "I just wanted to show you that I know where this is coming from, and that I know how old your history together is. That I know who you are. What you mean to my son." His eyes turn to his beer bottle, but he doesn't drink. "Did Luka tell you that I left them all, back then? That I just disappeared?"

"I know. That is, Luka told me you were gone for a few years." Dora is not ignorant of that. Still, it surprises her that he would bring it up. That he would mention it to her.

"It was terrible for all of them. For me, too, even though I was the one who left. But I found no peace. I had thought that the most responsible thing—for myself, for the children and, last but not least, for Antica—was to be true to my feelings." Zoran plays with the empty bottle. As if it were his life. It's always all or nothing. One or the other.

"I also think that we have responsibilities toward ourselves." Dora is not really in the mood to talk. She senses that something is off here. It sounds right, or at least almost right, but something is off. She wants to get up and leave. And stays seated.

"It didn't help anything. Or anybody. Antica committed suicide; Luka abandoned himself first, and then everyone else, and Ana grew up quickly, too quickly. I was alone and lonely. Everything should have turned out differently. I should have taken more care. A person has to make more of an effort. Not just give up."

Dora has an immediate reply: "When it's something that's worth the effort and trouble. Absolutely." She says the words emphatically. With so much passion that Zoran looks into her eyes and nods sadly.

"If only we could always know for sure when that is." He sounds

185

almost despairing. All at once, Dora knows exactly what's going on here, and what she needs to say.

"Luka and I are worth all the effort. We belong together." And with that, everything has been said that needs to be said. In Dora's opinion.

"Don't hold it against me, child, but I think everything should remain the way it is. You've got your life, Luka has his. Anything else would be too complicated." Zoran speaks gently, his voice is muted, as if he were embarrassed by his words. Just a little, but embarrassed, nonetheless.

"This isn't about easy or complicated. It's about two people who are soul mates." Dora is sure of herself, she's adamant.

"Soul mates. That's a nice word. Does such a thing actually exist?"

"Look at Luka and me. We're the answer to that question."

"It's so complicated. I think that easy is better." Pause. "Don't be mad at me."

"Zoran, nothing is easy about this, and it wouldn't be easy even if I disappeared. Especially not then. This wife of Luka's is blackmailing him. She's threatening to never let him see his daughter again. As if she could forbid him that—as if she were the only one who had a say." She gnaws her lower lip, and her eyes narrow into barely visible slits. She's angry. Ready to go to the barricades. "Is that the easy solution you're after? Do you really want your son to spend his life with a woman like that?"

Zoran makes no move to say anything. His head hangs low, as if it were the end of a long, draining workday. As if there'd been multiple double bookings, and he'd had to drum up lodgings for dozens of overflow guests in other hotels. He grips his beer glass tightly, then the bottle. Without drinking anything.

Dora slowly gets up. Suddenly completely calm. Almost motion-less. As if she'd given up, or as if she no longer cared. Or as if she'd already won. She looks at Zoran. Impartially. Objectively. She's got nothing to lose. So she permits herself to say she pities him. And then she goes. Crosses the terrace and down a few steps, off to the beach promenade. Donja Luka shimmers before her in the hot midday sun. She walks straight on, past the Yellow House, toward the lighthouse. Then she turns left, along the stony coast. To the rock.

Chapter 28

Luka wakes with a start. At first he doesn't know where he is. He's been dreaming. Not a good dream. And he's covered with sweat. It must be more than a hundred degrees in the room. Dora sleeps beside him. He looks at her lovingly. And with curiosity. Still with curiosity. Everything about her still surprises him. Everything he already knows about her, he loves. Anything he doesn't know he falls in love with as soon as he discovers it. But everything, absolutely everything, about her is familiar, as if he'd known it once before. Or many times before. Luka is insatiable when it comes to Dora.

He tries to get up without waking her. But the bed creaks. Dora murmurs incomprehensibly amid the folds of the sheet. Luka slips into the bathroom and closes the door behind him. He wants to take a shower, but not to make too much noise. Besides, he'd rather the two of them shower together. So he tiptoes to the balcony, hoping to catch a cool breeze. No chance. No mistral on this late afternoon. The sea is calm, so shiny and smooth that the water looks like oil. No movement anywhere. Everything sits and waits.

"Luka!" Dora calls out softly.

In one bound, he's beside her, which isn't difficult in such a small hotel room. This is where they meet whenever the room is free, which is often, luckily, because it's so tiny and understated. They've spent countless nights here. Savoring the sea. Silent along with it. Surrounded by pine trees that grant them rescuing shade. Too much light. When you've got secrets. When you don't want to be disturbed. When any other person is one person too many. When you feel more at ease at dusk. When you can touch every corner of the room from the bed.

"Dora," he whispers in her ear. In this minuscule hotel room. Which is like a whole universe. Like a whole life. Without borders. Endless. Infinite. Like the depths of the ocean. Unexplored. Full of secrets. Frightening. Irresistible. Fascinating. Like the stars in the sky. Countless. Unknown. Unsettling. Indestructible. Immortal.

"Luka!" Dora turns over onto her back and draws him to her. A kiss for the daily log.

"I was waiting for you, let's go take a shower."

"Why are you in such a hurry . . ."

And then they make love, and everything seems right with the world. The unsuspecting world, and Dora and Luka just as unsuspecting within it!

"Dora . . ."

"Yes?"

"I love you . . ." . . . only you always you my whole life long you are my breath my heartbeat you are infinite in me you are the sea that I see and the fish that I catch you have lured into my net you are my day and my night and the asphalt under my shoes and the tie around my neck and the skin on my body and the bones beneath my skin and my boat and my breakfast and my wine and my friends and my morning coffee and my paintings and my paintings and my wife in my heart and my wife my wife my wife my wife . . .

The unsuspecting world!

"And what happens now?"

Luka is silent. He doesn't want to say that he doesn't know. She knows that already.

"It can't keep on going like this."

"I love you."

"Is that enough?"

Luka stays silent. He doesn't want to say that he doesn't know. She knows that already.

"Why can't you leave her?"

Luka hangs his head. He feels miserable. Dora can see how tired he is, how torn, how exhausted by the battle between what he wants to do and what he is capable of doing. How this double life is wearing him down and humiliating him, sapping his energies.

"And don't tell me it's because of Katja. Nobody can stop you from taking care of your daughter, from seeing her. Nothing but hot air." Dora feels the anger building up inside her again. And how this conversation humiliates her again. She doesn't need this. It should be clear. Everything should be clear. Simple, Zoran would say.

"Maybe if you could be there . . ."

But this makes her furious. Because she understands. He doesn't have the guts to go through with it. It means nothing that he loves her. It's not enough.

"I can't take this anymore. I'm going to leave."

And then he holds her close, swears he'll never let that happen, tells her that she's his life, and that without her he will die. Dora doesn't have the strength to protest, she knows she would die if she could never feel his touch. Never see his eyes. Every day. All day long. Not to be loved by him. She wouldn't be able to bear it. It's plain and clear, and she has no real choice. She lets herself be embraced and comforted and convinced. And she stays. And they make love. And then they stroll through the town. Blatantly, holding hands. But Dora knows this is no victory. His home is not her home. At some point in the day, they must part ways, even if it's only so he can put on a clean shirt, or shave. It's Luka's wife who irons his shirts. The thought makes Dora sick. The world is so full of deception. It's a disgrace. One day they'll all turn into pillars of salt.

Dora and Luka both know that this is not the last discussion of this kind that they will have. So they remain continually on guard. They steal furtive looks at each other. They threaten to break up.

It should have been so simple.

Luka wakes with a start. At first he doesn't know where he is. He's been dreaming. Not a good dream. And he's covered with sweat. It must be more than a hundred degrees in the room. He feels a gentle, tentative touch on his back. Dora. He opens his eyes. In front of him a low table. In the corner a television. Next to it, a window with drawn curtains. It's dark. To the left of his head is an armchair. This is not a hotel room. That's obvious. He knows very well where he is. He's lying on the sofa in his own living room, and yet, he feels a hand on his back. It wanders. Cautiously. It's not Dora. It can't be. He leaps up from the couch. He's standing in his underwear, and Klara is still bent over the back of the sofa, looking at him. Luka recognizes the look, though he hasn't seen it in a long time, hasn't noticed it. She's wearing a gauzy red nightgown, and under it Luka can see her body, somewhat thickened by pregnancy. He averts his gaze. She straightens up, and says softly, "Luka." Her voice is throaty, full of the past, Luka recognizes the tone. But he's not interested. He's more scared than angry. "Luka," she says, and comes nearer. But Luka sticks his hand out in front of him, as if to protect himself, to ward her off. "You're still my husband, Luka," she says in silken tones, her lips barely moving. Luka takes a step back, his arm still outstretched. Then another step. He shakes his head. He doesn't want it. He doesn't want her. He doesn't want to humiliate her either. But she won't let him spare her. "Klara, stop it!" Nothing happens; she stands right in front of him, his hand is powerless. She leans her body against his and the room spins; he's nauseous, he takes another step back, says, "No, Klara, no, I don't want to!" But her hands are on his shoulders, her mouth rests on his chest, "No, Klara, no!" But she continues. "You are my husband, I love you, I want you." Her body now lies heavily against his, and he knows that soon he will have to give up. He knows he's about to throw up. He's afraid of losing consciousness. "No!" he screams, and doesn't care if anybody hears him, he feels like he has to fight for his life. He shoves her off him with all his strength, and she flies across the room, stumbles over the small coffee table and lands on the carpet in front of the sofa. She doesn't move. She just lies there. Luka strains to hear. It's dark in the room, it's still night. Nothing is moving. He's done it! Then he hears a soft whimper, a noise he usually associates with animals. Luka goes to Klara. "Klara, get up," he says, but nothing moves, he gets no answer. He looks at her, lying on the floor. Her nightgown is pulled up, he can see her legs and her naked backside. He feels nothing. It's as if he were dead. A feeling of humiliation slowly takes hold of him, and he hurries to the bathroom. He hangs his head over the sink, he can't risk an encounter with his reflection in the mirror. He drinks water from the tap. He can't stop. But then he does stop, because he's getting no air, though he lets the faucet keep flowing. He leans for support on the edge of the sink, and shakes his head violently, as if to rid himself of the images of what just happened. Once and for all.

Forever and ever. Dora.

He doesn't know how long he remains shut in the bathroom. When he opens the door and softly steps into the living room, it's empty. And it's light out. Luka dresses quickly and silently and leaves the apartment. He has only one thought.

Chapter 29

It happens at the beginning of September.

It's a fresh, sunny morning. Today Dora will lead a group of French tourists to Split, it's a day trip. She has to be at the harbor by nine A.M., where the bus will await her. Beforehand, she wants to go to the bakery to pick up fresh rolls for Aunt Marija and herself. Today they plan to have breakfast together, which they don't often get to do.

Still a little sleepy, she opens the front door. And there's Klara. Dora knows it at once. It can only be Klara. Just as it's written all over Dora that she's the woman Luka loves, so is it written all over this woman that she is Luka's wife. Even the ring on her finger bears his name.

Dora pauses for a moment, then starts walking. She has nothing to say to this woman.

"I want you to go. To leave Makarska, and to leave my husband alone."

Dora stops. She reflects for a moment. Then she turns around, standing tall, and faces Klara. They're about the same height. But Klara doesn't look good, she's gaunt, as if she'd lost too much weight too quickly, and pale, and her eyes are red and swollen. She's desperate. But Dora has no sympathy. She has to look out for herself.

"He loves me. Only me. That's never going to change."

"I'm the mother of his child."

"So what. He loves me. And he loves his daughter. And you should stop blackmailing him."

"He's my husband. He married me."

"Just because you were pregnant. How can you live with yourself?"

Klara starts to cry. This is too much for Dora. Besides, people are passing and gawking. They don't stop, they merely slow their pace as they pass the two women. Whispering. Heads touching. Dora feels like she's on a stage. But she doesn't like the feeling. She would like nothing better than for the curtain to fall.

"But I love him. What would I do without him?" Luckily, Klara speaks softly.

"Same here. And he belongs to me."

Dora looks at the other woman, whose face is contorted with pain and hatred. It's over. She's got to get out of here. And she'll take Luka with her. Here he will rot. Suffocate.

She runs away. She feels like she'll never be able to stop again.

In the evening, she returns from Split. Her tour group leaves the bus with happy faces. Dora gets big tips. She says good-bye to the driver, and the bus drives off. And there's Luka. And suddenly, everything she'd tried to forget all day comes back. Luka smiles at her faintly.

He's obviously exhausted and his shoulders hang dispiritedly. Dora wishes she hadn't gotten off the bus, but that it had taken her away with it. To the garage, if need be. Away from this hopelessness.

Luka hugs her without a word. Arm in arm they move away from the city and its lights. To the rock. A long silence, interrupted only by a few fleeting kisses. A feeling of powerlessness leads them forward like a trusty dog. Their steps are cautious. Sometimes tentative. And then they sit on the rock, their secret home. Where the past is as present as the current moment. Where their lives meet, and unite.

"Do you know that a few years ago they found a woman's body near here?"

"You're not serious! Was it a suicide?"

It had been a long day for Luka, too, apparently, because he just sits there, looking at her. The green of his eyes is murky, watery. Dora leans her cheek against his.

"No. Somebody killed her."

It's night already. The temperature is dropping. A cloudless sky. Soon it will be the full moon. The air is still. They sit, motionless, like figures in a painting on a museum wall.

"A murder . . . But it's so peaceful here."

"It was her husband. He called the police and turned himself in afterward. He'd wanted to get rid of her."

"Of course. What else."

Silence. Silence is known to be golden. Perhaps.

"Why are you telling me this?"

"The motive was love, it said so in the papers. I kept the clippings."

Luka speaks ever more slowly. It had been a long day, in every respect.

The moon shines bright. The water reflects its light. Somewhere in the blue darkness you can make out a pair of small fishing boats. Hear a motor. Oars dipping into the water. Life can't be held back.

The silence is magical, lovely, surreal. And even if life can't be held back, sometimes it seems to pause, and to stand still for hours, as if taking a rest. At such moments, you can take stock of yourself, as if seeing yourself through a telescope. You can look through one end of the glass and take in the big picture, or look through the other and observe yourself in minute detail. You can marvel. Or despair. Sigh. Congratulate yourself. Anything is possible.

"That's what it's usually about, love or money."

"He loved another woman, and his wife didn't want to let him go. He was desperate. He saw no other way out."

"And that was supposed to be it? The solution?"

"Well, it was, she was dead and he was free."

"Free? Didn't he end up in jail? He turned himself in, you said." Dora gets up, and walks across the rock, as if following an invisible pattern.

"Yes, but he got rid of her. He didn't have to turn himself in, did he?" Luka says it hesitantly, though it's not the first time the thought has come to him.

"Luka, what are you trying to tell me? I hope not what it sounds like."

"No, of course not." His answer comes too quickly.

"Luka!"

"We could do it, too, but without turning ourselves in! That would solve our problems!" Luka speaks quickly, insistently, until she interrupts him.

"Be quiet!"

. . .

Dora turns her back on Luka. She faces the sea. The stillness of the water. The lights. She closes her eyes. And, for the briefest instant in the history of time, she considers Luka's suggestion. It's inconceivable but liberating at the same time. As soothing as balm, and utterly impossible. Forbidden. Dora will never, ever admit to herself that she considered it at all, even for the briefest instant in the history of time.

"Dora?"

"Don't say a word. Don't ever bring this up again. And I'm going to pretend we've never discussed this. Never." Luka opens his mouth to contradict her. "Not one word. I mean it." Drained, Dora stands at the edge of the rock. "My life is not a Hollywood melodrama . . ." But she chokes back a sob, as if it were.

Luka musters the strength to stand up, and already he's beside her. He wants to embrace her, but she pushes him away, loses her balance. If he hadn't grabbed her in time, she would have fallen into the sea. She thinks of the dead woman and starts to cry. Luka takes her in his arms, and this time she lets him: She's too weak and confused to resist. And ashamed, if only secretly.

"Forgive me, please, forgive me, I don't know what came over me, I'm completely desperate, and I'm in such a terrible rage about me and Klara, she told me that she came to see you this morning, I'm so sorry, forgive me, I can't take this anymore; it's eating me up, I feel so helpless, absolutely powerless, forgive me, what I said, it's totally senseless, look at me, it's me, your Luka, only yours, nothing happened, trust me, forgive me, I just went crazy for a moment, I thought . . ."

It's not easy to say who holds whom now, and who keeps whom from falling. They stand on their rock, the picture of misery, watching each other fall apart.

· · ·

A few days go by. Everything seems to be back to normal. Dora and Luka spend every available moment together, they make love in the hotel room that belongs to them, even if they've never paid for it; or in the boat that's always at their disposal; or on the beach, which at night seems to exist only for them. They brew plans. They map out their life together in Paris. And Makarska. Because it's clear that they can't do without the sea. They consider where to live in Makarska, they'll need an apartment with a bedroom for Katja. And in Paris they'll have to rent a bigger apartment, because the current one has only one bedroom, so there's no room for Luka's daughter, whom they will want to have with them as often as possible. Parts will be auditioned for and won, prizes and distinctions accepted, paintings dreamed up, painted, exhibited and sold. And new children will be wished for, conceived and awaited with joy, and names thought up and scrutinized, then new ones found and discarded. And the whole time will be filled with love and desire. And laughter. Forever and ever, it goes without saying.

Everything seems to be going according to plan.

Still more days pass, and it's the nineteenth of September. Dora picks Luka up at the hotel at six o'clock. They want to go on a walk, Luka wants to show Dora a place where he'd like to paint a picture. He's only recently discovered it. Dora likes Luka's unbounded enthusiasm. The place isn't far off, just a short walk, past a few other hotels. Holding hands, they walk unhurriedly toward the campgrounds as Luka tells her about his day; stories of hapless hotel guests who can't figure out how the faucets work, or can't find the light switch, and swear that their lamps are broken. Dora laughs. Luka laughs along. Some people! Purposefully, but at their leisure, they draw near their destination. Only a couple of steps more, and they've arrived.

It's a small outcropping of land beneath the beach promenade, in the shade of a big, old leaning pine tree. Under the tree, well hidden, is a bench that once, long ago, was painted green. Today a few faded remnants of paint remain here and there. Rain, and the people who came here to relax, have left behind traces of their presence. Dora and Luka have sat here many times. They've even made love here. Ardently and quickly. With much giggling. The thrill of the illicit. But another time, Dora sat on the bench and read a book. Crickets chirped. Children squealed in the water. You could hear motorboats. It's a pretty and inviting place.

Luka jumps off the path and helps Dora climb down. He's not leading her to the bench, no. He ducks under the tree and positions himself on the edge of a little natural terrace. You can't see the promenade from the terrace, and you can't be seen yourself. Dora stands by Luka. She has to lean against him, because there isn't much room. Luka extends his hand and shows Dora what he wants to paint. With his thumb and index finger he makes a frame to show her what he's looking at. The perspective. Dora's hand glides across his back. She leans her head on his shoulder. Luka speaks in a voice full of enthusiasm, and when he pauses for breath, he gives Dora a kiss. The sun shines warmly, though it's sinking into the sea. The sea, in turn, dances to its own inimitable rhythm.

It's a beautiful day and a delightful place.

So Dora abducts Luka to the hotel. And is happy to find that the room they always take is occupied, so they have to take a different one. Because in a room that isn't their room, it's easier to talk. You can keep a cool head. You can speak without being afraid of what you might say. A hotel room is like a forgotten film set. Thousands of words stick to the walls, nibble at the mattress, lick the tiles in the bathroom, hang in the sheer curtains. You could persuade yourself of anything in such a place. Build yourself a new life. Tear it down. Kill yourself, without even noticing. Pretend it's all for the best. Convince yourself of that. Pretend you were convinced. In a room like this one. A room like any other.

"I'm leaving for Paris the day after tomorrow. Come with me."

"I can't."

"What are we going to do, then?"

"I can't keep this up."

"What does that mean?"

"I can't take it anymore."

"What do you mean by that?"

"I can't do it."

"You've chosen her?"

"I need peace."

"Instead of life?"

"I don't have the courage."

"Do you mean you're giving up on us?"

"It means I'm a coward."

"So you're letting me go."

"I want to die."

"That could happen to both of us."

"*Two happy lovers have no end, no death, / while they live they are born and die many times, / they contain nature's eternity.*"

"That is shit."

"That is Neruda."

"You have lost the right to recite Neruda."

"You are my life."

"Then you die."

"Dora."

"Forever and ever."

. . . you have to love yourself to grant yourself happiness to stay you have to be strong renouncing is easier giving up is easier suffering is easier . . .

"Dora."

Chapter 30

"Hurry, my darling! In a second we'll be engulfed by the masses, pure and simple, and we won't be able to see a thing!"

Helena is uneasy. She's standing at the door of Dora's bedroom and worrying. Not actually worrying that they'll arrive too late to the opening of the wrapped Pont Neuf. No. Given her daughter's emotional state, being on time means nothing to her. The Christo project is a big deal, a once-in-a-century event, for sure, but Dora means everything to her. And she is not doing well, not doing well at all. And that's an understatement.

Dora sits on her bed and stares into space. Her life is empty. The world is empty. And meaningless. And cruel. Superfluous. Useless. Dora's head is empty. No thoughts. They all left her three days ago. A couple of images remain, but with no associations. No observations or reflections. Feelings are not permitted. This is a deliberate choice. To feel nothing. Under any circumstances. Forbidden. Red danger lights blink, nonstop. At one point, Dora isn't sure if she's breathing.

She probably is. She looks at her rib cage, yes, it's moving, so breathing is happening. But she doesn't feel it. She hears her mother speak. She can't make out the meaning of the words. Dora is absent. From her life, which has ceased to exist. She doesn't even want to die. She has no desires and no will. All she can do now is wait. Wait for life to find her again. That could take a while, because she has hidden herself very well.

Luka sits on the living room sofa and stares into space. His life is empty. The world is empty. And meaningless. And cruel. Superfluous. Useless. Luka's head is empty. No thoughts. They all left him three days ago. A couple of images remain, but with no associations. No observations or reflections. Feelings are not permitted. This is a deliberate choice. To feel nothing. Under any circumstances. Forbidden. Red danger lights blink, nonstop. At one point, Luka isn't sure if he's breathing. He probably is. He looks at his rib cage, yes, it's moving, so breathing is happening. But he doesn't feel it. He hadn't counted. He definitely would have remembered that. But it's not necessary to pass out either. Luka is already absent, anyway. From his life, which has ceased to exist. He doesn't even want to die. He has no desires and no will. All he can do now is wait. Not for life to find him again. No, that's not going to happen anymore. That's gone. Departed. Flown away three days ago. Life is over. He'd wanted to give up on life, and find peace instead. That was the deal. But it could take a while before he actually finds peace. It has hidden itself well. Or Luka has.

"Come to bed, Luka!"

Or maybe not so well hidden!

Of course, Luka doesn't answer. Soon Klara is standing beside him, laying her hand on his shoulder.

"Come to bed, it's late."

She knows. Everybody knows.

Where can he go? This damned city! Every corner full of ghosts.

Luka slowly gets up without looking at his wife. He puts on his shoes, which are by the couch, picks up his wallet, which is lying on the table, and leaves the house without a word. Klara calls after him. He closes the door behind him softly, carefully, even, and walks and walks, apparently aimlessly, farther and farther. Suddenly the boat is in front of him, bobbing on the water. Not so aimless, after all. It's easy to deceive oneself. He jumps on board. Unlocks the cabin and lies down on the berth. Below, in a drawer, is a T-shirt that belongs neither to him nor to his father nor to Ana. It's a white T-shirt with a red-and-blue symbol on it. Something Chinese, supposedly. It's a T-shirt that belongs to nobody who's in Makarska now. It's just there, and he likes knowing it's there, even if he won't get it out of the drawer. He couldn't bear to. He can't bear to be reminded of the life that hides within him. Can't bear to look at pictures. But to lurk on the fringes of life—that he must do. Luka is a master at punishing himself. As his glance travels around the cabin, he sees his paint box and lets out a short cry. He grabs the old box, meaning to throw it into the sea, but it breaks apart in his hands. Brushes and paints and cloths and tubes and mixing glasses land on the floor. Blind with rage, he rampages around and picks up every single scrap and throws it all out of the cabin. Some bits reach the calm, nighttime waters, others land, clattering, on the deck. Life is over. He's not going to paint anymore. He doesn't deserve to. Painting is a gift of life. And he is dead.

Sweating and shaking, Luka sits on the cabin steps and weeps.

Chapter 31

While the whole world exults or marvels or anguishes about the reunification of the two German states, Dora and Jeanne sit on the second floor of the Eiffel Tower at one of the most expensive restaurants in Paris, Le Jules Verne, toasting Dora's twenty-eighth birthday. The year is 1990.

"Here's to you, my dear! And to many more years as successful as this one!"

Jeanne's cheeks are flushed, she doesn't have much of a tolerance for alcohol, one glass of wine and she has to struggle to remember her own name. So Dora looks out for her, one glass will do. She's only drinking at all because it's Dora's birthday, and because Dora won two awards this year and last week began rehearsals for her new play, so there's a lot for them to celebrate. It's a dream role for Dora, one that's always been at the top of her list: Maggie in the Tennessee Williams play *Cat on a Hot Tin Roof*. Philippe Dédieu will play Brick, that makes her happy. She knows Philippe from the Academy, he was in the final year when she was just starting out, and she

saw almost all of his performances at the Academy. For a while afterward, he'd vanished from the Paris stage, he'd gone to New York and
tried to get a career going there, but a year ago, he'd returned to
Paris, where he'd performed a brilliant Hamlet. And now they are
going to act together. Dora is incredibly excited. The previous Friday,
Philippe and Dora had met for a glass of wine after rehearsal. There
had been hunger in his eyes, Dora told Jeanne the next morning, and
couldn't help giggling, like a schoolgirl after her first kiss. Jeanne
giggled with her. As usual. They were still best friends, just as they'd
been ages ago, on the bench in the Parc Monceau. "You're falling in
love with him," Jeanne crowed, and Dora said, "Don't be ridiculous,"
and then they started laughing again and throwing pillows at each
other. Like two little kittens, playful and silly.

"Thank you, Jeanne." Dora drinks her wine slowly, savoring every
swallow, and every bite of the delicious morsels tastefully arranged on
her plate. It's a feast for the eyes and the palate, an expensive one, but
today that doesn't matter. She's still alive and she's doing well and she's
successful and can afford a meal like this. In any case. She looks out
at the city beneath them, and is filled with a deep feeling of peace. But
also excitement. And above all, gratitude. She's still alive. Even if
there are certain subjects and things that she still regards as off-limits,
particularly certain names, an eye color, a smile. Strictly secret. Memories of fingers and lips. Dora suddenly finds it hard to breathe.

"What is it, Dora?"

"Nothing, it's just . . . nothing."

Jeanne looks at her warily. She knows, of course, what's on Dora's
mind. It's always the same thing. The tiniest thing can set off Dora's
train of thought. Jeanne is worried. After five years, you'd think . . .
But no, not with Dora. Nothing has changed. Nothing.

And yet, life is full of surprises. In the blink of an eye, a good-looking man is standing beside their table, and Dora can smile again.

"Philippe!"

Philippe bends down and gives Dora a prolonged kiss on the cheek. Jeanne notices that Dora closes her eyes, as if she wants to disappear into this kiss.

"That was a good catch!"

Luka nods silently while Vinko lights a cigarette. The cooler is full of fish, it will bring in a lot of money. Vinko takes off his cap and scratches his head.

"I hate this cap. It itches so much!"

"Better than frozen ears."

"Or frozen hair." Vinko puts his cap back on.

"Not something you need to worry about, my friend!"

Vinko acts like he's going to give Luka a punch, and the two of them crack up. They're having a good time, they're laid back, relaxed. Luka is happy. This is how it ought to be. No turning back. These days he thinks more and more about his father, and about the time when he took off, just disappeared, taking the boat with him. Back then, Luka had suffered, but now he understands why his father left, and wishes he could do it himself, vanish into thin air, or melt into the water. Without a trace. Because sometimes this peace he chose is simply unbearable. Sometimes life catches him off guard, tackles him head-on, fills him with pain and euphoria and longing, and then he has to flee. To the sea. Away. So he doesn't have to count, so he can breathe. Especially now that Ana's gone, too—two years ago, she suddenly decided she wanted to study, medicine, no less!—so now nobody's around to worry about him and his breathing. He can't afford to take chances. Now he runs away from it all. That's his new strategy: to bolt, without ever escaping. But at least the illusion of escape remains, an attempt. To break out and catch a fleeting breath of life, only to go home again.

"What will you do with the money? Buy yourself a new hat?"

"Very funny. Really." Vinko stubs out his cigarette and flicks the butt into an empty beer can. There are piles of beer cans, because you never want to skimp on beer.

"No, seriously. What will you do with it?"

"Biserka thinks we should finally get married."

"And you?"

"I don't have to get married." Vinko leans his head back and looks up at the sky. "No, my friend, everything can stay just as it is."

"You won't get away with it, you know."

"Yeah, I know, but I'm going to hold out as long as I can. That's allowed, isn't it?"

"Keep dreaming, my friend, as much as you want, as long as you can. But I've heard that she's already looked at wedding gowns."

"Oh, man!" Vinko moans with exaggerated despair, and Luka smiles.

"Or you could volunteer to go up to the mountains, and clear logs from the streets of Lika . . ."

"Those crazy Serbs! Blockading the roads with logs? What are they thinking?"

"It's just a provocation, my friend, nothing more than a provocation. We should ignore them."

"That's easier said than done. When a log pops up in the street in front of you, you can't get past it. Mato told me it's no laughing matter, he came back from Zagreb last week. There's definitely nothing to laugh about . . ."

For a while, they fall silent.

"Do you think there might be a war?" Luka looks at his friend.

"I don't know, with people this crazy, anything is possible, it doesn't look good."

"Oh, man, I hope they'll find a way to work things out before this log revolution escalates."

"Yeah, that would have to be a crash course in diplomacy. I've got a feeling time is running out."

"You're probably right. Look at the two of us, we're as clueless as these fish in the cooler."

Vinko laughs, lights another cigarette and takes a generous swig of beer. They're having a good time, the male bonding that Luka enjoys so much. Luka's feeling great. Until he leans his head back, like Vinko's just done, looks up into the night sky and sees the clouds. It makes him dizzy. But he can't stop himself, he's got to keep staring at them, as if his life depends on it. Without realizing it, he lets out a cry.

"What is it, Luka?"

Vinko knows his friend. And he knows the story, which must not be mentioned. He sees the pain in his friend's eyes, alternating with absolute emptiness, or anger, or hopelessness. But he also knows that he must not say anything. Has to pretend that nothing's wrong, to act as if he didn't notice anything. All he can do, really, is be there for him, keep him from being alone and keep an eye on him. Distract him.

"How does Katja like kindergarten?"

Abruptly, Luka is back. Yanked from the shapeless clouds. Luka meets Vinko's glance. He has to struggle to keep up his end of the conversation.

"Good," he says. The answer comes slowly. "She likes being with other kids. She cries when we pick her up. The teacher says that's never happened before."

"And what's Klara up to?"

"She's trying to start up a dancing school again, I think. This time, it's supposedly actually going to work out. There are still a couple of forms to fill out, authorizations and signatures to get, and then it'll be good to go."

"That's great."

"Definitely."

"And Dora?"

"Today is her birthday."

When the birthday girl wakes up the morning after her celebration, she has a mild headache and a bad taste in her mouth. Dora reaches for the water bottle beside her bed, but there isn't one. She opens her eyes, and immediately realizes she's not in her bedroom, and not in her own bed. Cautiously she turns her head toward the other side of the bed. Damn it! She had always told herself, had vowed, to never get involved with a fellow actor during a production. Never. You must wait until everything is completely over—preproduction, rehearsals, all the performances—before you even think about spending a magical night or two with some Orestes or Antony. And now this! Damn it again! The role means too much to her for her to have compromised it this way. And yet, she really likes Philippe. Something clicked between the two of them, even the first time they met. And the sex wasn't bad at all, no, she had to grant him that! That is, as far as she can remember, given that she was a little tipsy at the time. But still. You ought to at least obey your own rules. Laws are made to be broken, but not the ones you make for yourself! What would this lead to?

Dora slips carefully and very softly out of the bed, hoping it won't creak, or make some other noise. Made it! She quickly gathers her clothes and leaves the bedroom. Skipping the bathroom, she gets dressed in the hallway. Quickly, quickly. As her hand grips the doorknob, she hears Philippe's voice: "Dora, Dora, where are you?" The voice is coming closer. In the nick of time, she flees. Once more, a lucky escape!

Tonight she will have to face him, onstage. But that's doesn't matter. She can take cover behind Maggie.

Luka sits in his bar drinking wine. His head hangs over his glass, as if he were searching for gold in it. The room is full. People, music, laughter, shouting, the clinking of bottles and glasses.

"Luka, there you are!" Vinko bellows across the room to make his voice heard. Luka raises his head and looks at him a little dazedly, and Vinko immediately knows that his best friend has already had too much to drink. "Here, this is Sanja, Biserka's friend from Dubrovnik. Say hello to Sanja."

"Hello, Sanja!" Luka says politely, and looks at the young woman between Vinko and Biserka. Sanja is short, but her hair is wonderfully black and her eyes are dark, and in the condition he's in, Luka can imagine she's anything he wants her to be. Which he does. The picture isn't distinct, which makes things a lot easier. He can see what he wants to see. Which he does. Sanja doesn't smile all that innocently, more like she's got saucy ideas on her mind. She sits next to Luka and takes a sip from his glass.

Vinko and Biserka look at each other doubtfully. Vinko looks around. Klara is nowhere to be seen. Not that that surprises him. When his glance returns to Luka and Sanja, her left hand is already on his upper thigh, and his right hand is on her neck. Their noses are so close together that you couldn't slide a finger between them. Vinko looks questioningly at his girlfriend—who would much rather be his wife—and she answers with a helpless shrug. By now, Luka and Sanja have already managed to mash their lips together.

It's all the same, Luka thinks in his muddled head. I'll just keep on going the way I did before life came calling. Who does it hurt, it's all the same . . . And then they're outdoors, heading toward the beach. It's all the same.

And not even a month after her twenty-eighth birthday, Dora learns that she's pregnant.

Chapter 32

Two weeks before Christmas, Dora is woken in the middle of the night by sharp stomach pains. In the bathroom, blood flows down her legs in thin stripes, like tinsel. It's over. She doesn't cry. It was a crazy idea, anyway. She drives alone to the hospital. It's over. There's nobody for her to tell.

As she returns to consciousness, after many hours of drugged sleep, everything seems blurry. Thoughts and feelings, names and faces. Her eyes are dry, but her cheeks are wet. It's over, and anything could still happen. A stormy sea suffuses the emptiness of her body and her soul, salty foam envelops her like a second skin.

Now what?

Dora calls Jeanne. She wants to leave the hospital, but the doctor has advised her to stay at least one night. But she can't. Tonight she has rehearsals, and she absolutely must be there. Because she has a plan.

Before the doctor will sign her release papers, he tries to cheer her up one more time, telling her that she's still young, that it's not unusual, especially because it's her first pregnancy. He says many other kind things, but Dora isn't paying attention. She has a plan. She nods agreeably and smiles like a pro, and then Jeanne comes and gets her and drives her home. She helps Dora into bed, sits beside her and strokes her tangled, tousled hair. Dora's dark eyes stare at her gravely. "You really ought to stay home today," Jeanne says, "you can go to rehearsal tomorrow." Dora moves her head, but it's impossible to say if she's nodding yes or shaking her head no. Dora is very quiet. As if it had nothing to do with her. As if she had a plan. And, guess what, she does!

Before she falls asleep, she whispers, happy and relieved, "I'm going to go visit Luka." And then she's out. Visiting her dreams.

Chapter 33

It's the first time in almost six years. This gorgeous city on a perfect bay. At the foot of a tall mountain that you can climb, if you feel like it. The sea everywhere. It shimmers silver in the morning sun, like eternity. Like the house of God. Dora sits on the bus, tired and excited, and is overcome. By the view, by her great anticipation of what she's about to see. Her eyes get wet and she hides them behind big black sunglasses. It's a cold but sunny day in February. The year is 1991. Aunt Marija has been dead for three years, so no more chocolate cake. Only Luka remains. But that should be enough.

A beautiful young woman. At the reception desk. In tight jeans and a thick, blue winter jacket. Flat, elegant winter shoes. A small traveling bag. A dark blue purse. Hands hidden inside red mittens. Long, curly hair. Unruly. It gets in her eyes. She keeps blowing it away. A narrow, pale face. As if it had never chanced to see the sun. Full lips. A wide nose. Big, dark eyes.

Dora.

. . .

"Dora."

And Luka is already counting: one, two, three, four . . . and Dora quickly finds the way behind the reception desk, and presses her body against his. She can't quite feel him through her thick coat, but she presses her mouth on his, and whispers softly to him: "You are my prince, don't fall asleep, stay with me, look at me, look into my eyes, my prince, I'm here, everything's fine, my prince." Luka sinks into the swivel chair beside him as if he has no muscles. No will. As if he were one of those old, holey air mattresses that always turn up in unexpected places at the hotel, left behind by their departed owners. His eyes are closed and his breathing is labored. There are some things in life that you're never prepared for. He feels Dora's head on his stomach, her arms around his waist, but oxygen is in short supply at the moment, so he keeps sitting there, motionless. He feels the pressure of her body, and it's strange and wonderful at the same time, and he wants both to hold on to her and to push her away. He opens one eye, he has no strength for anything more, and sees her in front of him, on her knees, her long hair in his lap, and the happiness overwhelms him and crushes him at the same time. He hears her murmur, her voice doesn't quite reach him, but it might be the word "prince" that leaves her mouth. He lays his hand on her hair.

Dora recovers herself and raises her head. Her eyes are moist, and her lips move, forming the word he'd anticipated, and Dora knows that Luka knows that he has lost. Is lost. Because he's won: She's there, and whatever happened is now over, and now the cards are being reshuffled, even if he doesn't know about it, and she can tell already that she's holding trumps, she can only win, which means

Luka will win, too. Has already won. Everything is to be expected. Because Dora has a plan.

"Let's get out of here."

"It's so empty here!"

"The hotel is closed. It's on winter hiatus until April."

"What are you doing here, then?"

"Waiting for you."

"Right. And besides that?"

"I had to sort through some documents—proposals, inquiries, paperwork."

"Then, it looks like I lucked out."

"No, I'm the one who got the lucky break."

"You might want to wait a bit before you say that."

"There's nothing to wait for, you're here."

"That's true."

"Thank you."

"It's out of pure selfishness, not a trace of altruism is involved."

"That doesn't matter."

"Luka."

"Dora."

"I love you."

"Thank you for coming."

"You're welcome."

"How long are you staying this time?"

"How long would you like me to?"

"Don't make me answer that."

"It can be as long as you want."

"Dora."

· · ·

Everything is the way it always has been when the two of them are together. Perfectly right. Their movements in sync. Everything merges. Seamlessly. Bodies, glances, words. Life's perfection. As if no intervening time had separated them. As if there had never been another time.

For a week, Dora occupies a small room in the closed-down hotel, Luka's is the only other warm body in it. It's cold. The chill north wind, the *bura*, shrieks through the abandoned hallways and rooms. The air is as clear and sharp as a shard of broken glass. You have to turn your head away from the wind to breathe. The sea is like a sea urchin, it pierces with every touch.

Dora and Luka are not apart for one instant. They make love, they either eat at the restaurant on the beach, where they are the only customers, or they have picnics someplace in the hotel, at the bar, in front of reception, in the breakfast room where, unfortunately, no breakfast is served, in the big hotel kitchen where there's nothing to eat; they go walking down the desolate streets that flank the beach, to the rock. The rock is a good place in this weather, it shields them, the wind can't reach it because it's on the southern side of the Saint Petar peninsula. Dora and Luka sit here, wrapped in a blanket from the hotel, and make love, their teeth chattering. They talk a lot. They have a lot of catching up to do. Dora tells him about her successes, and about Helena, who's split up with Marc, and Ivan, who's made a comeback and is courting Helena with undreamed-of energy. He's making a fool of himself, pure and simple, Helena complains, but really she has nothing against it. Dora can mimic her mother so well, so exquisitely, that Luka can't help laughing. Dora talks about Jeanne, who's still working with disabled children, and is thinking of going to Africa, there's so much misery everywhere. Dora says not a word about the men in her life, because they're not important. Nor does she let slip a word about her miscarriage. Or her plan. Which is working wonderfully so far.

Luka tells her about all of his disappointments. Nothing but failures. He'll turn thirty-two this year, hasn't painted in almost six years, and never will again, that's what he's decided; still works at the reception desk, will never quit the job, that's what he's decided. Luka can't hide the contempt he feels for himself. Dora holds him tight. She is shattered, speechless. A life that tries with all its strength to destroy itself. Dora feels like screaming. So much denial and waste and self-punishment—and for no reason. Dora is distraught. She holds Luka tight, and Luka says not a word about all the women who've had Dora's name, or Dora's face, which pushes his wretchedness toward absurdity.

They cling to each other, defying the darkness, the cold, the wind, the dread of Dora's departure. Today, already. Because tonight is the last night.

"No other, my love, will sleep with my dreams."

Hundreds, thousands, of responses come to Dora's mind, but none is worthy of Neruda, not even Shakespeare. She fights the tears that become more urgent with every moment. February nights are long and dark, and the morning seems as if it will never come. That's the only consolation they have. The hope that the sun will forget to rise. Why not? Anything is possible.

"Luka," Dora whispers. "I want you to be happy. To take better care of yourself."

"Darling Dora."

"Please. Otherwise all of this sacrifice was for nothing."

"I don't want to. I don't know how to be happy without you. Without you . . . I don't deserve it." Luka's voice, close to desperation, hurts her.

"But somebody has to gain something from our unhappiness!"

"Katja. Katja gets something out of it."

"Maybe." Dora ponders. "But she'd get more out of it if her father were happy."

Silence.

"I never say your name out loud. I can't even think it."

"It's the same for me."

"I couldn't bear it."

"I would die."

"And that would be inexcusable, such a talent!"

"Exactly! And for the same reason, you've got to paint again. The world misses you, Luka."

"Dora."

"We have to make the most of this opportunity, where everything is permitted, even the unimaginable."

"In order to love you, my love leads two lives. / So that I can love you when I don't love you / and love you when I love you."

"You're crazy."

When at last the sun shyly sends out its first rays across Makarska and the sea, Dora gets up, dresses quietly, looks over at the sleeping Luka, does nothing to still her beating heart, breaks down and leans against the wall for support as the world whirls around her like a carousel. She can't move her legs, her feet don't want to leave the room: Because life is here.

Dora presses her lips against Luka's forehead.

"Luka," she whispers for the last time.

She leaves the room.

And Luka opens his eyes, which hurt from this game of pretending to be asleep. But he has promised her not to wake up, not to get up with her, or to make love to her one more time, or embrace her. I wouldn't survive it, Dora told him, in a dry voice that had threatened to crack at any moment. He had to promise not to accompany her, not to watch her leave, or wave good-bye. She has permitted him nothing. Except to play dead.

"Dora," he whispers for the last time, before the floodgates close for good. "Dor . . ." And then it's over and done with.

Chapter 34

Dora sits in the airplane. The Alps beneath her. She lays a hand on her belly and smiles. You've always got to have a plan, then nothing can go wrong. She had calculated everything precisely. It just has to go well. It had been the right days, the absolutely best days. It must have worked.

She refuses a glass of wine. You can't start being careful early enough. "Cheers," she whispers, and drinks an orange juice. Not half bad. She drinks a toast to herself, and to the man whose name she must go back to not speaking anymore, and to Love and its fruits— forbidden or not: She is the only one who gets to decide.

Closing her eyes, she leans back in her uncomfortable airplane seat. She's dead and alive at the same time, everything and nothing at once. The pain isn't lessened by the altitude, the memories aren't blurred, and hopefully she is . . .

She smiles. In her handbag she has a painting by Luka. A portrait of her. In it, she's sleeping. Her head lies on her outstretched right arm. Her left hand rests on a sheet that touches her face. She looks contented. Serene. As if she were having beautiful dreams. A strand of hair lies across her left cheek. You can see her bare shoulder. You can see that she is pregnant. Clearly and distinctly. Luka painted it without seeing it. He painted into the picture the truth that he will never learn.

Luka hasn't been this drunk in a long time. Vinko can hardly hold him up. He half carries, half drags him home, while Luka shouts incoherently that he wants to be taken to the hotel, that he's got a room there, that's where he lives now; or to the boat, that's his home. Then he throws up. That's how it goes, the whole, endless, long way home. Vinko takes Luka's key and lets them in. Everything is quiet in the apartment, only light snoring comes from one of the rooms. It's already two in the morning. Vinko lays Luka on the living room couch, covers him with the blanket draped over the armchair and goes home. There's nothing more he can do for his best friend. Dora is gone. Everything is gone. That's the story of Luka's life. Vinko shakes his head sadly. He's glad he's got his Biserka.

Luka is awoken by a horrendous headache. He groans. What a night! He tries, with as little movement as possible, to turn around. Dora. He opens his eyes. The light is blinding. He closes his eyes again. No. Dora's gone. Departed. Now he's alone again. Dead. Whose bed is that, then? It's not the hotel room. It's also not the berth in the cabin, and it's not the sofa in the living room. He opens his eyes again. But the bed isn't so unfamiliar after all. Nor is the room. Nor is the woman next to him. He shuts his eyes again. Red alert! Damn it! How drunk was he, to have been capable of doing something like this, and not remember? Luka feels his stomach heave, he runs to the bathroom, clings to the toilet bowl like a life preserver. He throws up and cries.

Eventually he leaves the bathroom and drags his heavy legs into the living room. He sits on the couch. This is his bed when he sleeps in the apartment. Which only happens by accident. His aching head lies in his hands, the nausea returns. He almost believes it'll never go away again. Which would be okay with him. He deserves it. To have betrayed Dora this way. He stands up quickly, hurries to the bathroom again, resumes his devotions to the toilet seat. He will be true to it; it's a deep-sworn vow. He dares to leave the bathroom only after a long while.

Klara is standing in front of him. Happy. Beaming. Pleased with herself. She snuggles up to him. "Thank you," she whispers, "it was wonderful, I'm so happy that we're back together and that everything will be the way it used to be, I've missed you so much, you can hardly imagine, all these years without you, but tonight you showed me that you do still love me, and . . ."

Luka pushes her away. Urgently, and furiously. "You raped me," he screams, "I hate you, I will never again in my life touch you, you repulse me, you took advantage of me, the state I was in, you saw I was totally drunk and devastated, how could you, not even a man would do a thing like that, you are the worst, what was I thinking, oh God, how could you do a thing like this to me, I think I'm going to throw up again . . ."

"Papa!" Katja is standing behind Klara, almost completely hidden by her. "Papa!" And then she cries and beats her face with her tiny hands. "Papa!"

Luka goes into the bathroom and bolts the door.

Chapter 35

Late in the evening of November 5, 1991, Dora brings Luka's son into the world. Everything happens quickly and without complications. Mother and son are healthy and well. Helena, Ivan and Jeanne sit in the waiting room, and toast the new arrival with champagne that Ivan brought with him. He'd even thought to bring glasses. Helena looks at him gratefully, and he nods at her lovingly. Since Helena left Marc, Ivan has regained a little of his former charm, he takes more trouble with his appearance, has even bought himself a whole wardrobe of new suits. His eyes sparkle again, and he smiles more often. Helena says he reminds her of the young man she married, way back when, a hundred years ago, and laughs coquettishly, fluttering her eyelashes.

"To Dora!" says Jeanne, who's flying to Zimbabwe a couple of days later, just before Christmas, to tend to needy, sick children. She has tears in her eyes. It's simply too much—Dora, the baby, her move, everything so new and uncertain.

"To my grandson!" Helena says, and cries, sobs and laughs; and then, because she doesn't know how she feels or what she should make of all of this, she cries a little more and daintily blows her nose in the handkerchief Ivan holds out to her.

"To love!" Ivan says, surprising even himself with the declaration. But at moments like this, it seems to him that love really is the most important thing in the world, and that everything ought to revolve around it. He looks at Helena, the woman he's never stopped loving, and thinks of his daughter, who was crazy and headstrong enough to do all this on her own, to take hold of what she wanted, who'd done everything out of love for one man, and still does, and who, from what he knows of her, will never do any different. Then suddenly he has to swallow loudly, and his eyes fill with tears of pride at having the privilege to be her father. He can't have done everything wrong if he's produced a daughter like this.

And then they're permitted to visit Dora and her son. They hurry. As if it were an award.

Luka sits in his corner at his local bar, and drinks his third glass of wine. He doesn't know why, but tonight he's in the mood for wine. Red wine. As if there were something to celebrate. Today is a very special day. Without knowing why, Luka smiles, grins and, from time to time, closes his eyes, as if he were seeing pictures. And he really is. For a moment, he longs for a canvas and paint, because the picture in his head is fantastic, he's not worthy of it, and yet, there it is in his head, fully formed. Does that mean something?

"The next round is on me!" he shouts to Ante, the waiter. There aren't many people there, but all of them know Luka, and thank him loudly and profusely. Luka returns his attention to his glass and to the picture in his head and is content. If he were bolder, he could even be happy. But contentment isn't bad either. He doesn't understand what's up with him. He simply has an incomprehensible, groundless feeling that at this very moment, while he's carelessly wasting his nonprecious time in this bar, something important is happening, something of single importance to him, something he doesn't have the courage to dream of even when he's alone on his boat in the middle of the sea, or when he's drunk. And this unknown something lightens his heart and his soul and he feels like he could paint again. It's a miracle, and Luka is grateful, without knowing what for.

"Why are you grinning like an idiot?" Vinko is standing by Luka's table, looking at him suspiciously.

"No reason. I don't know."

"And buying a round for everybody, there's also no reason for that?"

Luka realizes his friend is upset. Put out. "Yeah, why not? Things are good with me."

"You're aware that your wife has been in labor for a whole day, and that things are getting dangerous, right?"

"Maybe so. But that has nothing to do with me." Luka regrets the words as soon as they leave his mouth, even though it's how he feels, and he thinks he's entitled to them.

"And does it also have nothing to do with you that the damned Serbs have besieged Dubrovnik and are firing on Šibenik? Luka, what's wrong with you?"

"Nothing." Luka sticks his nose in his glass.

"I hardly recognize you anymore."

"You're in good company there, my friend."

"Luka, will you finally grow up!"

"Let's drink and keep quiet."

"This is about your wife and your baby!"

"So it is. As if I could forget. As if anybody would let me forget about it."

Vinko looks at Luka with visible scorn and shakes his head.

"Biserka sent me to find you and tell you that things aren't looking good. That you should go to the hospital." And he starts to walk away from Luka's table.

"Vinko!"

"What?"

Indecision.

"Oh, nothing." And then suddenly it occurs to him that Klara might die, and that he would be freed of the misery he alone had imposed upon himself. Suddenly he feels a kind of hope that he has not felt for years, and feels no shame at the thought. No. He even dares—he's become so cocky all of a sudden—to whisper Dora's name into the nearly empty wineglass.

"His name is Nikola."

Dora glows like a tree on Christmas Eve. She's a little pale, that's all. Her eyes glisten and she can't stop smiling. The deed is done.

"That's a gorgeous name, *Dorrie*! Gorgeous, pure and simple!"

Now it's real, forever and ever. Just like they'd promised each other. Even if that promise was broken. But it doesn't matter anymore. Because she was the first woman in his life. And she has his first son, and his first paintings. The works. Now she's got everything.

Except for him.

"Luka! Luka!"

Someone calls loudly and knocks on the door of the cabin. Luka doesn't fully wake up, he's had too much wine and too much hope, a rare combination for him.

"Luka! Open the door, my son!"

It can only be Zoran, but Luka can't open his eyes, much less the door. "Luka! Are you there? Luka! Come on, open up, it's important!"

The noise and the shouting don't die down, so Luka slides out of the berth and crawls blindly toward the door.

"Hi, what's up?" Luka tries to smile, to seem hospitable.

"What are you doing here? Your wife is in the hospital, and you should be there, too." Zoran stands at the door. Luka throws himself back onto the berth and closes his eyes.

"Luka, my son, what's wrong?"

"I don't know, but it was something good, for a change."

"That's true enough, you've had a little girl! Another daughter, my son! You ought to be at the hospital."

"No, I don't think so."

"But I do! Luka, they're not doing well . . ." Zoran's voice breaks. Luka opens his eyes.

"What's happened?" And although nobody would be able to hear it in his voice, Luka knows he's filled with an awful, hopeful yearning.

"Klara is doing reasonably well, but the little one is having terrible difficulties, she couldn't breathe, then immediately went into cardiac arrest . . ." Zoran weeps. "The doctors don't know if she'll make it . . ."

"She stole her. It doesn't surprise me. Thieving never brings luck." Still, he feels a pain in his gut, the force of which surprises him. Is that the hope that's dying?

"What are you talking about? Who stole what? Luka!"

"Klara stole this baby like a wicked thief, she's the most wicked thief there is. Nothing good could come from that." Luka is not angry, and not spiteful. Pain slowly and thoroughly courses through his body. All at once, he's completely sober.

"I don't understand a . . ."

"Never mind, Papa. Let's go to the hospital." To see the thief and her loot, he thinks.

The next day, Luka signs up for the Croatian Army. Two weeks later he's sent to the war zone of Dubrovnik.

In and around the besieged city, seven hundred Croatian soldiers and policemen fight against thirty thousand Serbian and Montenegrin soldiers. Isn't that just great.

Chapter 36

In the early morning of July 3, 1992, nearly a year into the Siege of Dubrovnik, Luka is wounded, one day before a major onslaught by the military operation Tiger, in which the Croatian Army will try to take back the western and northern regions around the city and secure the traffic on the Adriatic magistral.

He's lying behind a rock and observing enemy lines through a telescope. Everything is quiet. And then suddenly there's a blast, and he screams and his leg bleeds, and he can see his bones and he faints. He doesn't even have time to count.

In the early morning of July 3, 1992, Dora wakes with a faint cry. It's 5:20 A.M. Nikola sleeps beside her, quiet and full. Her nightgown is damp and her hair sticks to her head with sweat. She can hardly breathe, and she starts to sob. She wants to stand up, but her legs won't support her, and she has to sit down on the bed again. Laying her hand on her rib cage, she massages it with slow, circular movements. She tries to do breathing exercises, but she can't manage it, she's distracted. Now she remembers what made her wake up. She'd been dreaming. Luka was standing in front of her, he was smiling. But he was smeared with blood, a lot of blood. You couldn't see anything but blood. And his smiling face. Then he fell to the ground, where he remained. He couldn't move, could only smile.

Dora cries. Softly, but intensely. She lies down in bed again and takes Nikola in her arms. He sucks happily on his tongue and keeps on sleeping. He can't think of a better place to be in the whole world than in his mom's arms.

"Luka, my prince, my Luka, only mine, forever and ever," Dora whispers and weeps as she holds Luka's son tightly in her arm.

Luka hears a gentle voice next to his face. "You are my sleeping beauty, only mine, wake up, you are my prince, only mine, I'm here, everything is all right, wake up, look at me." Then other voices and words reach his ears, and, confused and weak, he opens his eyes and sees Dora's face. His lips move without making a sound, but he can't say anything, so he smiles faintly, and she smiles, too, and he shakily raises his arm and stretches his hand toward her face, and he touches her long black hair, and she whispers once again very softly, so softly that only her lips move and only he can hear: "You are my prince . . ."

At last, Dora falls asleep. She doesn't dream. Her sleep is an endless emptiness without light, without water and without oxygen. A person cannot survive in this emptiness. Yet Dora wants to stay there, for fear of living a life without a happily ever after. She cries in her sleep. Then Nikola's cheerful babbling wakes her, and she knows that she will stay alive until the very end.

.   .   .

Nataša Dragnić

Luka spends two weeks in an overcrowded hospital in Split. Everything goes well. The leg can be saved. He might end up with a bit of a limp. But that's practically nothing, Zoran says, and squeezes Luka's hand. He keeps looking at him, he can't get enough of his son. He has to keep touching him, to reassure himself that he's still there, that he's doing well and that the thing with his leg will work itself out, the main thing is that he's still alive, and it's over. His son belongs to him again, and everything is the way it ought to be. He can breathe deeply and relax, and now he'll be able to sleep soundly again. He'll spend a whole week just sleeping. The main thing is that Luka is there. Healthy and in one piece, and with all his limbs. With a stiff or shortened or crooked leg, but who cares about that?

At the end of July, Luka returns home.

Klara stands at the door with the baby in her arms. Katja hops up and down beside her and cries, "Papa, Papa!" and runs in circles. Luka steps out of the car; he doesn't want Zoran to help him. He leans on his stick for support: He'll never again be without it. Katja keeps calling for him, and pulls at his hand. He laughs. "Not so fast, Katja, Papa can't go so fast, his leg hurts." He walks, pulled into the house by his older daughter. Past Klara. Without a word. Past the baby in Klara's arms. Without a glance. Zoran turns away from this misery, quickly wipes his face.

For Luka the war is over, but the nightmare continues. In every sense.

For weeks, Dora has nightmares, can't sleep, thinks that Death lies beside her in bed. She hardly eats a thing, she has trouble breathing. Helena insists she go to the doctor, but Dora refuses. She's afraid that the doctor will find nothing wrong with her, and then she will know with absolute certainty that something has happened to Luka, and she could not bear it. She holds tightly to Nikola. He's her anchor and her life preserver. Dora waits. There's nothing else she can do.

And what do you know! One day, it's all over! The nightmares, insomnia and breathing problems disappear as unexpectedly and suddenly as they arrived. And she goes with Helena and Nikola to her favorite café on the Rue Sainte-Anne and orders three pieces of chocolate cake with whipped cream, and eats them up without once putting down her fork. Helena laughs with tears of joy. Nikola thumps his plastic cup on the table and crows with pleasure.

In the evening, she goes to the theater again and works enthusiastically and with exuberant high spirits, almost a little hysterically. But nobody complains, everyone is happy she's back. Especially Roger, her director, who would like to be more than just her director. And Chekhov is happy that his Irina has rejoined the other two sisters.

When she comes home at night and takes Nikola from Helena's arms, she kisses the sleeping child and whispers, "Everything's just as it should be, *moje zlato*, everything's great, and Dad's doing fine."

Chapter 37

"There, a dancing bear, and he's wearing a big hat. Can you see him, Mom?" Nikola is excited. His outstretched arm doesn't move, even though the wind makes the clouds roll past quickly, so they don't hold their shapes for long.

"Of course! And did you spot the little ball in his hand?" Dora takes Nikola's hand and gives it a long kiss.

"Bears don't have hands, Mom, they have paws!" Nikola laughs at his mother's ignorance.

"You don't say, my love? How lucky that you're here to clue me in!" Dora strokes his black curls. "But I also see a dancing shark, with a rose in his snout. I think he's going to invite the bear to dance a tango, what do you think?"

Nikola laughs in delight.

"Mom, that's impossible! How could they ever meet?"

"But, you know, bears love water, it won't be a problem, believe me." And Nikola laughs again, loudly. Passersby look at them and smile.

He and Dora are lying on the lawn in the rose garden of the Parc
Monceau. It's Nikola's favorite place. He likes the scent of the roses,
and likes to hear stories about his mother's childhood that take place
in this park, or in a small harbor town by the sea, where he hasn't been
yet, but where Mom has promised to take him sometime. He can't
hear enough about Papou—oh, how he wishes he could have a dog!—
but Mom says their apartment is too small, a dog has to have a yard—
or about her adventurous trips on the boat, or about the secret rock,
and the delicious chocolate ice cream. Nikola loves ice cream. Especially when it's as hot out as it is today, and when he's on summer
vacation, also like today. Nikola doesn't like going to school. He likes
to see his friends there, but he doesn't like the teacher at all. She's
mean to him a lot of the time, just because his mom is a famous
actress. Nikola thinks that's totally unfair. But also, he's not especially
interested in the things they teach him at school. He wants to be a
captain one day. On a great big ship. He wants to study the seas and
oceans, and learn about fish and whales and, especially, sharks.
Sharks are his favorite animals. And not only the big, well-known
ones, no, he likes the cookiecutter shark best, which lives only in deep
water, or the hammerhead shark, because it's so ugly and Nikola feels
sorry for it. He imagines the other sharks laughing at the hammerhead, and making fun of it. It makes no difference that the hammerhead has sharper senses than the other sharks, and can maneuver
better than they can. That's just the way sharks are, they make fun of
anyone who's different. But Nikola's main task as a shark expert will
be to find the megalodon, the biggest shark in the history of sharks—
between thirteen and fifteen yards long—to find it and to prove that
it's not extinct.

Dora sneaks a sideways look at her son and marvels. How did he get so big so quickly? Only yesterday he was her baby, and now he's almost ten years old, soon he will leave her, go off to college, get married. Or plunge under water in a cage to look at man-eating sharks! Dora tries not to cry, but it's hard for her to imagine her darling son eye to eye with a great white shark.

"Mom, what's wrong?" Nikola's little hand touches Dora's cheek.

"Nothing, sweetheart, I've just been staring at the clouds too long."

"Should we go home?" Nikola asks, a little let down.

"We could go get an ice cream," Dora slowly replies, as if she had to give the matter serious thought.

"Or two!" Nikola is laughing already.

"And tonight I don't have to go to the theater, so we can go visit Grandma and Grandpa in the country, and have dinner in the garden. What do you say to that?"

Nikola jumps up and hugs his mother so fervently that Dora nearly starts crying again.

"Thank you, Mommy, thank you! You are the best mommy in the world!" Nikola smothers her with kisses, and they end up lying on the grass again and laughing like a couple of five-year-olds.

"And we really should thank Roger, because he was so nice and gave Mommy a night off."

"Roger is also the best! I like Roger," Nikola whispers into Dora's ear.

"Me, too," she whispers back.

Luka sits on the beach watching his daughter, who's almost ten years old and is sitting in the sea and playing with stones. Again and again she turns and looks at him. She doesn't smile. She rarely smiles. She just looks at him, as if to ask: "Why are you still here?"

Luka sits in the shade, because even though it's already six o'clock at night, the sun is still too hot for him. Not for Maja, no. His younger daughter loves the sun and can't get enough of it. For that reason, Luka goes with her to the beach when most of the tourists are already at dinner, if he's not on his shift. He simply sits and watches her. It calms him. Like a kind of meditation. He watches the sun, the sea, the emptying beach, the sagging pine trees. His daughter. She's doing fine. She made it. Things didn't always look good, but the worst times are over. They've still got to keep an eye on her, she can't tire herself out too much, and she still has to take a couple of medications, but what is that compared to the catastrophe at the beginning, when she nearly died.

And now she's splashing around in the sea, looking at him sternly. She's never learned to swim. Didn't ever want to. At first, Luka had pressured her, but then he left her alone. Not everyone has to know how to swim. After all, his mother didn't.

"Papa, why can't animals laugh?"

His daughter Maja.

It's a lovely, warm summer evening. It stays light until late. The year is 2001. Dora and Nikola speed along the road to Versailles, to the place where Ivan had built a little house for him and Helena five years earlier. After Helena had accepted his proposal again, and Nikola had carried the rings, looking like a black-haired angel. As Helena put it, life had come full circle, pure and simple. And at that moment of familial happiness, Dora had reflected upon her own life. Would it become a circle, or remain a straight line? Then she looked at her son, and made a wish for everything to turn out for the best, whatever that might mean.

"Mom, will we be there soon?" Nikola is sitting in the backseat, reading his book. *Killer Sharks*. What else?

"Yes, darling."

"Mom, did you know that a shark has a blowhole, like a whale?"

"No, you don't say."

"But it's not on top of their heads, it's at the side, near the eye." Nikola doesn't raise his glance for one second from the book, which is bigger than his thigh.

"Really? That's fascinating." Dora watches her son in the rearview mirror.

"Mom, are there plays about sharks?" Now he's looking at her, too, their glances meet in the mirror. He looks earnest and thoughtful.

"Not as far as I know. But I can look into it if it's important to you. Roger would definitely know." She isn't laughing. She's impressed.

"I don't know. Would you want to play a shark?" He doesn't break eye contact with her.

"I don't know. What kind of shark did you have in mind? You know your mom is pretty picky when it comes to which roles she wants to play." She gives him a wink.

"Of course it would be a special shark, the prettiest and smartest and happiest shark of all time. And it would be the main character, of course." Nikola is very happy with this new role he's created for his mother. He knows what she likes. He's been going to her premieres for years already, and never gets bored, even though he mostly doesn't understand what's going on, because he loves watching his mother onstage, seeing how she transforms herself. Becomes somebody else, while remaining his mother.

"We're here, look! Grandpa's already out there waiting for you!"

Dora stops the car, and almost at the same time, Nikola's already outside and running to his grandpa. Ivan crouches down, and as Nikola crashes into him, the two of them tumble onto the lawn, chuckling. Nikola laughs and closes his eyes. Helena appears at the door, claps her hands and calls out to her grandson. He leaps off his grandfather and runs to his grandmother. Hugs and kisses without end. As if they were a proper French family.

"You would think it's been forever since you've seen each other!" Dora laughs and helps her father to his feet. He's not so young anymore. Dora doesn't want to think about it, she tries to overlook both the subtle and the more obvious signs of aging in her parents. Otherwise it would make her sad. And Dora is magnificent at repression.

"Hello, Dora." Ivan hugs her.

"Hello, Papa." Dora surrenders to his hug. It's like being wrapped in security.

"Mommy, where is *my* papa?"

Nikola is standing near them, Helena behind him. His big eyes are filled with confusion. Everyone looks at Dora. And Dora sees Nikola's father in front of her and smiles. But Nikola's glance takes on a dark, brooding cast, as it does from time to time, which sometimes spreads to his thoughts and feelings. Even his actions. But nothing changes.

Luka brought Maja home, she was tired. Now he takes his daily walk, and hopes he won't run into Katja and her boyfriend. He grins. Katja would be furious with him. She wants to keep her big love affair secret, even though the whole city knows about it, because Andrija is a boy she went to kindergarten with, and the two of them were best friends until they grew older and discovered they were in love with each other. From the age of six, whenever Katja was asked what she wanted to be when she grew up, she had answered without hesitation, "A wife and mother." And now, at sixteen, to be a wife and mother is still the height of her ambition. That doesn't bother Luka. Whatever makes her happy is fine with him. Nevertheless, it's been a continual source of disagreement between mother and daughter. But now that it's obvious that Andrija is here to stay, Klara has gone silent. As if she'd given up. Perhaps she is reminded of another romance when she sees the two of them together. Certainly, many other people make that connection, even if they talk about it only in hushed whispers.

Ana, who has just opened a gynecology practice in Makarska, is rapturous about the young romance, and thinks with insatiable longing of Toni, who wasn't as lucky as Luka, and died in the Siege of Dubrovnik. Ana also has to think of Dora when she sees her niece with her boyfriend. And she asks herself if they were all wrong back then when they pressured Dora to go away. Ana isn't sure, she knows only that love is a sacred thing. Especially if you're forced to renounce it. She also sees that her brother isn't happy, he never made it. So many lives were wasted. And that's why it makes her happy to see Katja so radiant with joy.

Luka avoids thinking about anything connected with the past. He's learned to survive, that will have to be enough. He's got the children, he's got his boat, his father is still healthy, his sister is back. What he doesn't have he doesn't think about. He just goes on walking with his cane. That has to suffice.

At the lighthouse he meets Vinko and Lovre, Vinko's son. They are deep in conversation, even though Lovre is only five years old. They don't notice Luka at first, and Luka enjoys the scene. Father and son. He wishes he had a son. But maybe he'll have a grandson one of these days. It looks like Katja's in a hurry.

"Luka, are you sleepwalking or what?" Vinko waves him over. "Come look what we've found!"

"I found it, it's my money!" Lovre shouts, because there are too many grown-ups around all of a sudden. And everyone knows how liable grown-ups are to come up with stupid ideas. Like, for instance, that you should give back cool things that you find, or hand them over to the police. Which Lovre is not inclined to do. Before much longer, he'll have to start crying, he can tell. So he says emphatically once again, "It's mine, I found it, it's mine!"

Luka comes nearer, smiles at Lovre, who eyes him mistrustfully, and sees a shirt lying on a rock, a wallet in Vinko's hand. And he thinks back to the murdered woman, and wonders why he hadn't done the deed himself back then. Thoughts, memories and emotions strike so suddenly! What can you do to guard yourself against them?

"Do you think something bad happened? Who leaves his shirt and his wallet just lying out like that?" Vinko looks anxiously at Luka.

And Luka thinks about what a fraud he is: He'd never even had the guts to *leave* Klara—how could he ever have brought himself to kill her? Breathing and suffering, nothing else remains.

"Do you remember the murdered woman?"

Chapter 38

"She needs a new kidney, and pretty quickly. The second pregnancy should never have happened." The doctor speaks detachedly and disinterestedly to the family gathered around him. Everyone is there, even Luka, who ordinarily prefers to skip the hospital appointments.

Ana is there, and speaks with the doctor in the unintelligible lingo that has meaning only for the initiated. Zoran and Maja play chess. Maja wins. She's the smartest one in the family, it's as if she'd come into the world old and wise. Katja's husband, Andrija, stands beside the doctor and Ana and hangs on their every word, without understanding anything, but he's there, he's got everything under control, nothing bad can happen. Klara sits on the hard hospital chair and stares into space. Luka stands at the window and thinks of the night when Katja was born. And he knows what he has to do. Slowly, his leg trailing after him, he goes up to the doctor and makes a suggestion.

"Good, of course that's always the best solution. But we have to make sure first that your kidney will be accepted by the patient."

"Why wouldn't she accept it? I'm her father!" Luka finds it ridiculous and outrageous.

"Of course. Nevertheless, we have to do some tests first."

Again Luka wants to protest, but Ana takes his hand and draws him away. "Everything is all right, Luka, everything is all right," she whispers to him. She leads him to Zoran and Maja, and Luka sits down with them and is silent. Zoran purses his lips to indicate fellow feeling. Luka lays his hand on Maja's head. She looks at him, wonderingly and a little suspiciously, as always. "Everything will be all right, Papa," she says, and returns to plotting her next move. Andrija sits down beside Luka. Luka grins at him and nods as if to say, "Yes, I know, it's rough, but everything will turn out just fine." Andrija looks at him, and Luka can see fear and anger and helplessness in his young eyes, which have yet to behold misfortune or sorrow or failure.

"Where are the kids?"

"With my mother."

"Good."

Then a long silence, full of uncertainty. The only sound is the movement of the chess pieces across the wooden board. The year is 2008.

"Mom, what do you think of it?"

"It's wonderful! Or maybe . . . a bit too dark and menacing? Did you draw it yourself or did you copy it from a book?"

"I painted it myself, of course."

"It looks so real, so alive, you'd think it could suddenly attack and bite you. Fascinating!"

"Yes, isn't it? It's a snaggletooth shark, *Hemipristis elongatus*. It lives in the Indo-Pacific region and in the Indian Ocean, all the way to the Red Sea. Not very big, four feet long, maximum. Do you think Monsieur Demy will be happy with my presentation?"

"You have a great talent, my son. Maybe you should give painting a try."

"Maybe."

"Why did you walk in weather like this, Papa? Andrija could have picked you up." Katja wipes the raindrops from Luka's face.

Luka lets her do it, he likes her touch on his skin. It feels nice. Nobody touches him anymore, not for years. Not since he stopped, many years ago, fooling around with more-or-less random women whom he met in bars. A person can get by without sex. But he feels old and used up and worn out, even though he's only forty-nine.

"Oh, it doesn't bother me. You know, I need my exercise, and it's just a few raindrops!"

Katja shakes her head in displeasure, as if he were a disobedient child who makes his mother worry.

"How are you doing, sweetheart?" Luka holds her hand.

"I'm fine." But it's obvious that she's not. Katja is pale, with bluish circles under her eyes, and her skin is damp, even though she wasn't out walking in the rain. And she still has a temperature. Luka asks himself why these tests have to take so long.

Right on cue, Ana appears at the door. She smiles at her niece, and waves Luka over to come to her.

"What is it?"

They're standing in front of Katja's hospital room. Ana shuts the door. Luka has a bad feeling, but doesn't know why.

"Luka, I'm sorry." Ana clearly doesn't know how or where to begin.

"Is it about Katja? Has she run out of time? Does she need to be operated on immediately?" Luka wavers between fear and anger and an urge to take action.

"No, it's not about that. It's not about Katja." Ana's face is contorted with awkwardness. It pains her, it's obvious that she is having this conversation against her will.

"Ana, what is it? Tell me, finally!"

Ana looks at him as if she needs to beg his forgiveness. Her eyes grow wet and redden. She takes his hand and Luka lets her.

"Ana!"

"I am so sorry . . ."

"What is it, for God's sake, tell me!"

Ana wipes tears from her eyes. She hugs him and holds him tight.

"You are not Katja's father," she whispers in his ear, and as Luka faints and slides to the floor, she can't hold him up and falls down with him, and lies beside him. On the hospital's cold linoleum floor.

Over the next few days, Nikola industriously paints and draws. Only sharks and other sea creatures, but still, it's something. His portfolio grows, filled with wonderful pictures that are so realistic you almost take fright when you look at the animals, and nevertheless want to leap into the blue-green water.

Dora takes the portfolio and visits her old friend Christian, who now owns two galleries in Paris and one in Berlin. They haven't seen much of each other over the years, but whenever they do meet up, it's always with deep feelings of mutual sympathy and affection. Now Dora wants Christian's professional opinion of her son's paintings. She is curious if he will recognize the father in the son's work.

"There you are! It's been ages, hasn't it!" Christian hugs her warmly and kisses her three times. He looks great, as if he were in the early days of a new love affair, which is likely the case. Christian falls in love several times a year, generally with a pretty young artist whose paintings he then exhibits, rarely with much success. Afterward, he has a habit of saying that art and business must be kept strictly separate from affairs of the heart. Until the next time, of course.

"Yes, *mon ami*, we say that every time we meet, and nothing ever changes." Dora smiles and lays her hand on his cheek, as if she had wanted to pat it.

"At least I get to see you regularly on the stage, I'm at every one of your opening nights, and I have to tell you, I worship your Blanche DuBois, I think it's better than Vivien Leigh's."

"Thanks, that would really be something!"

"Well, it's not like you didn't win an award for it, there's no need to act so humble, I know you!"

"Then, you know that I'm anything but humble, my friend!"

And they laugh merrily. Neither of them mentions Luka, just like all the times before.

"So, show me, what do you have for me? You're being so mysterious!"

Dora opens up the portfolio on the big table in Christian's office, takes out the pictures and lays them beside one another. Then she takes a step back to give Christian time. Which he takes. In full. He looks at some of the drawings and paintings longer than the rest, turns back to others a second time. As he does this, he moves his lips as if he were silently talking to himself. His whole face is in motion, reflective, hunting for clues, groping its way forward. At one moment, he closes his eyes, lets his head fall back and draws his hands through his thinning hair. Then he groans like a marathon runner after he's reached the finish line, opens his eyes and looks at Dora. Thoughtfully, very thoughtfully. And a little warily.

"What is this?" he asks then, pointing a finger at her accusingly. But before Dora can say anything, he disappears into a room behind his office and stays there for a long time. Dora sits on his work stool and begins to spin. "Will we ever grow up?" she asks herself gleefully. Then she hears whooping sounds coming from the room into which Christian has disappeared.

"What's going on?"

She's about to get up and go to him when he appears in the doorway. In his hands he holds a small canvas.

"Here, I knew it immediately."

Dora looks at him suspiciously.

"Well, not immediately, but now, in any case, I feel sure. Here, look here!"

And Christian shows Dora an oil painting, a small study of the sea and its inhabitants. He puts it among the paintings Dora brought him.

"So, do you get it?"

"Yes, I get it. He is his father's son." Pause. "But he's afraid. Look out for him. Maybe they should . . ."

"Don't say anything."

It wasn't easy, but Luka has made it. He sits on the rock, which hasn't changed noticeably in the last seventeen years. Everything is still there. The small pine tree, which doesn't look as if it's grown any bigger. The countless creepy-crawlies that certainly aren't the same ones as back then, but look as if they could be. The smoothness of the stone, refreshing and warm at the same time. The sea. Eternal. Blue, green, gray, turquoise.

Luka takes a deep breath. No, he won't faint, he won't start counting. There is something more important he's got to do. Something he's even more afraid of. And yet, he's certain that he's going to do it. To make a decision. No, not to make it, it's been made already. But to carry it out, that is what he must do now.

Luka lies down on the cool stone. He looks at the sky. There are no clouds. The whole sky is a steel-gray canvas. Beside him lie his walking stick and a rucksack. In the rucksack is the Neruda book. In Spanish, of course. Apart from that, there's a sketch pad and painting tools. Brushes, colors, mixing glasses, cloths, sponges. Everything that belongs there. His heart seizes up at the mere thought of what he's about to do, as if he has a cramp, and he feels like crying. Long and bitterly, with stored up disappointment and resentment. And yet underneath it all lies the hidden hope for something, for a life that he'd stopped daring to dream of. For many years now. Decades. And then he becomes aware of the fear attached to this hope.

For several days, the world has looked different. No longer is he father of his daughter, for whom he had renounced his life. He'd been tricked, deceived, robbed.

When he had fled from the hospital a few days before, he had run home—if you could call his hobbling gait a run—and shut himself in the basement. For a long time he'd sat there, on a shaky old chair. He'd breathed. For hours. He was very happy with his breathing. In and out, deep and slow. Practice makes perfect! In and out. With closed eyes. At some point, when it had already grown dark, he had stood up, and, with great deliberation, gone to the back end of the cellar, where he had not gone for decades, and yet, he'd known instantly where he would find what he was looking for. Two big trunks. He'd carried them to the chair and into the light, sat back down, and continued his breathing exercises. Gathered his courage.

Then Luka had opened the first trunk. Paints, sketchbooks, sketches, pencils, cloths, smaller canvases, unfinished paintings. The smell of happiness. Of self-fulfillment. Tears flowed down his cheeks, irrepressible and unchecked. His fingers shook impatiently and fearfully. Can a person lose his talent? Forget it? What if he can't paint anymore? What if his ability has disappeared? Neglected. Mistreated. Luka had rubbed his hands on his old, faded jeans. For a long time, he contemplated the open chest. He knew what was inside it, yet he couldn't bring himself to shove it to the side. He wanted it to remain in front of him. A memory. An impetus. The power source for the next hours and days. For the moment that was fast approaching. For the second trunk.

The second trunk. Full of photos. Shells. A couple of rocks. Mozartkugeln chocolate wrappers. Kid stuff. Drawings. Three books of Spanish poems. Paintings. Bills. The second trunk, filled with memories that had waited sixteen years—some of them twenty-two years—to be handled again. Experienced. Loved. In the moment that Luka saw Dora's photograph, he had to stand up and open the window. Her voice in his head. He laughed and cried, and started to count: one, two, three, four, five . . . He heard a gentle voice next to his face. "You are my sleeping beauty, only mine, wake up, we'll get married now, you are my prince, only mine . . ."

Yes, that's how it will be, he had thought, and closed the cellar window.

Luka sits up. It's growing dark out on the rock. He takes up his

Nataša Dragnić

sketch pad and his pencils. He looks around. The pine tree. Why not? His fingers toy with the pencil, as if they want to perform a trick. Holding the pencil feels good, it rests comfortably in his hand, like it belongs there. Luka draws the first stroke, then another. Quickly and decisively. As if the cellar years had never happened. With each line, Luka grows. And with him, his resolve. And the confidence that anything can still happen, that everything is still possible.

That somebody else has to save Katja now. And will.

That he can now paint again, unrestrainedly.

That he will find Dora.

That it's not too late for anything.

And he doesn't want to waste any thoughts or emotion on Klara. Never again. He has no time for questions and explanations. He has just been granted a reprieve. That's enough for him.

Soon the painting will be done.

Then it will be time for Dora. And his life.

Dora can't fall asleep. Thoughts that she doesn't understand occupy her head, and spread throughout her body disguised as feelings. She lies quietly in bed and doesn't sleep. Her eyes are open. What she sees she doesn't fully understand. Her thoughts address her, but she can't grasp the meaning of what they are trying to say. Everything seems confusing to her. But these jumbled messages pester her, leave her no peace and finally force her to get up. She goes to her study, to the massive old armoire. She stands in front of it, trembling in her thin nightgown. Crouching down, she pulls out the lowest drawer. It sticks. It hasn't been opened in almost two decades. It takes a great deal of strength and agility to dislodge, she pulls it, then jiggles it, then pulls again until she lands on her back on the hardwood floor.

252

But the drawer has been conquered, and at last is open. In it are only two boxes. Dora looks at them a long time, she can't decide whether to touch them, much less to open them. She could put together an inventory list of their contents without casting a single glance inside. Her life is inside. Her life as it should have been. Everything is in it. Gone, and yet still there. Forever and ever. Ripped violently from her. Taken away. Stolen. But never forgotten.

Dora sits on the hardwood floor in her study, trembling on this cold November night, and feels the world change shape before her eyes. As in a time-lapse nature film. In which nobody marvels to see a beautiful, full-blown rose emerge from a seed in the space of a few seconds. Everything stays the same at first glance, but you can still sense the transformation, throughout your whole body. The heart beats more quickly and irregularly. And not because of the financial crisis. It's closer to a shift like global warming. Vital. Existentially important. Something that affects the whole universe.

Dora doesn't cry. She does breathing exercises. In, out. You've got to do it at least three times if you want to really calm yourself down. In, out. In, out.

"Dora."

In, out.

"Dora!"

"I'm coming!"

And Dora gets up, closes the drawer with her foot without having touched the two boxes, leaves her room and closes the door behind her.

She knows what she has to do. It's decided.

Chapter 39

L uka looks at the unfamiliar woman who's just entered the lobby. He doesn't know her. He's never seen her here. Her black hair, short and wavy. And shiny. Like the glittering blue-black scales of a mackerel, a fish that must keep in constant motion or it will sink. She enters the room as if she owns it. As if it were stage. She's tall and slender, and full of movement, even when she doesn't move—and he can't take his eyes off her.

Dora enters the hotel lobby hopefully. It's the third one she's tried. Because the Hotel Park has closed. Many others, too. But this has to be the one. Hotel Dalmacija. A tall, thick-set man sits at the bar, a walking stick by his side. He talks easily with the underoccupied bartender, while the bartender checks her out. That doesn't bother Dora. She's used to it. She takes off her heavy winter coat. Her eyes meet the glance of the other man. He's playing with his stick, and Dora thinks he's really too young for a walking stick. Or for gray hair. Then her head suddenly starts to swim, it feels full and hollow and blown up like a balloon, and dizzy and hot and light and fluttery and transparent. She closes her eyes. She stands still. Pictures come to her in waves. They wash over her. And nobody's there to ask her what's wrong.

Luka doesn't move. He leans against the bar counter, and holds his breath. He's afraid that if he relaxes his muscles and breathes, the unfamiliar woman might disappear. He fixates on her until it hurts, and his eyes begin to tear up. Then his consciousness dissolves into nothing and he slides to the floor. He hasn't even had the time to count. Slowly he disappears. Like the entries in the reservations book, whose pages he slowly flips through.

Dora is the first to come to the side of the man who fainted. She has seen this once before. Twice, actually. She has witnessed it. And she knows what to do. So she crouches beside him, tinier than tiny. Her eyes widen, until her face, paler than pale, seems to be nothing but eyes. She bends her head over the man's, and, before the bartender or the receptionist can kneel at his other side and raise his legs, kisses his pale red mouth. And nobody is there to call out her name in dismay.

Luka hears a soft voice next to his face. "You are my sleeping beauty, only mine, wake up, you are my prince, my gray-haired prince, only mine . . ." Then other voices and words reach his ears, until, confused and weak, he opens his eyes and . . .

. . . she sees his eyes, opening slowly, his distraught expression, his lips that move without making a sound . . .

. . .

. . . but he can say nothing, so he smiles faintly and . . .

. . . she smiles, too, and . . .

. . . he shakily raises his arm, stretches his hand toward her face, touches her short, black hair, in which he now can see a couple of silver strands, and . . .

. . . she whispers once again very softly, so softly that only her lips move and only he can hear: "You are my prince."

"You came."
    "Yes."
    "I called for you."
    "I know."
    "You heard me."
    "Yes."
    "I love you."
    "And I'm married."

Chapter 40

"It's hard to believe."

  "What is?"

  "That I'm here."

"Why?"

"After so many years."

"It's nice."

"Like sleeping in your own bed after a long trip."

"I know."

"Like tasting something you haven't tasted since childhood."

"Those round, white lollipops."

"With the picture in the middle."

"And the colored border."

A waterfall of memories. A small hotel room in the heat of summer. Pine trees that grant rescuing shade. Too much light. When you've got secrets. When you don't want to be disturbed. When any other person is one person too many. When you feel more at ease at dusk. When you can touch every corner of the room from the bed.

"Hardly anything has changed here."

"You think?"

"I can still picture you."

"But without gray hair and without a walking stick."

"How are you?"

"The nightmares hardly come anymore."

"That's good."

"Yes."

"Why are you smiling?"

"Because I can still picture you as well."

A beautiful young woman. At the reception desk. In a tight, dark blue dress. Flat white sandals. Two big trunks. A white handbag. Fingers full of rings. Long, curly hair. Unruly. It gets in her eyes. She keeps blowing it away. Blue-white earrings. A narrow face. Full lips. A wide nose. Big, dark eyes. Impatient hands. An elegant watch.

"I forgot about my work."

"When?"

"When you came into the lobby."

"When?"

"Back then. Don't you remember?"

"I don't need to remember."

"And seeing you is . . ."

". . . like a dream."

". . . like Christmas."

"And Easter."

"And birthdays."

"And the first day of spring."

"All together."

Their bodies next to each other. Sweaty. Tired. Hungry. Insatiable. Happy. On damp sheets. A hand on the stomach. A fingernail on an upper arm. Mouth on breast. Leg over hip. His green eyes.

"Have you thought of me?"

"How many times, my love, did I love you without seeing you, and perhaps without memory, / without recognizing your glance, without beholding you."

"I'd almost forgotten."

"What?"

"You and your Neruda."

"I imagined . . ."

"What?"

"Life with you."

". . ."

"Forever and ever."

"And?"

"It was full of wonder."

The tiny hotel room. Like a whole universe. Like a whole life. Without borders. Endless. Infinite. Like the depths of the ocean. Unexplored. Full of secrets. Frightening. Irresistible. Fascinating. Like the number of stars in the sky. Unknown. Unsettling. Indestructible. Immortal.

"How is your daughter?"

"I have two."

"Congratulations."

"Thank you."

"No, I thank you."

"What for?"

"Just because."

"Why?"

"Forget it."

"I don't want to forget."

"Have it your way."

"Do you have children?"

"A son."

"How old?"

"Seventeen."

"Seventeen?"

"Yes."

"I wonder . . ."

"What?"

"So, a son."

"Yes."

"I . . ."

. . . love you only you always you my whole life long you are my breath my heartbeat you are infinite in me you are the sea that I see and the fish that I catch you have lured into my net you are my day and my night and the asphalt under my shoes and the tie around my neck and the skin on my body and the bones beneath my skin and my boat and my breakfast and my wine and my friends and my morning coffee and my paintings and my paintings and my wife in my heart and my wife my wife my wife my wife . . .

"I've got to go now."

"Please don't."

"Why not?"

"It's cruel."

"What is?"

"To come, and then to go."

"I have no choice."

"A person always has a choice."

"It's ironic that you would say that."

"I was weak."

"Yes, you were."

"I've never gotten over it."

"Tough luck."

"I've never stopped loving you."

"I believe you."

"I want you to stay here."

"It's too late."

"Who has ever loved as we do?"

Once upon a time there was a little hotel by the sea, sheltered by pines from the cold north wind. Its southern wall tasted of salt and heat even in winter. Big windows and balcony doors reflected the waves. The sea wrapped itself around the small pebble beach like the night sky filled with stars. Where everything began. And there they lived, happily ever after. Where everything should end.

"Look, the clouds!"

"Do you remember?"

"And do you?"

Chapter 41

And so, from the winter garden, they look for a moment at the clouds, a final curtain for their memories. A bridge to the present.

"A sailing ship in a storm, there on the left."

"Yes, the sails are whipping in the wind."

"Exactly." Dora looks at Luka in wonder. "That's the first time we've ever agreed! Can it be?"

"Obviously—you finally grew up."

They sit in comfortable wicker chairs, side by side. Luka holds Dora's hand. And until this moment, everything else is irrelevant. Their bliss at each other's proximity is still so overwhelming that it drowns out anything else.

"I've never played this game with anyone else." His voice sounds dreamy, even a little proud.

"I have. With my son." Dora tries to dodge his gaze, but he doesn't give her the chance.

"Tell me about him."

"Why? What do you want to know?"

"Everything."

Dora finally looks at him, and Luka knows what he wants to know. He smiles at her and squeezes her hand, as if he wanted to say, "Come on, tell me everything, I have a right to know, and you know it." Dora twists her mouth, as if in defeat.

"His name is Nikola, he's seventeen years old, he wants to be an oceanographer and we recently discovered his talent for painting." With each word she speaks about her son, her face becomes a little more radiant. As if she were growing alongside him.

"Sounds wonderful."

"He is wonderful!"

And they can't help laughing at this surfeit of parental pride.

"What does his father do?" Luka asks, as if incidentally.

"Lives." Short and sweet. There's no need to say more, Dora thinks.

"Interesting. Good for him."

"You could say so."

"When was he born?"

"He's seventeen years old. Can't you do the math?"

"I mean, on which day? When is his birthday?"

"Why?" Cautiously, even a little combatively.

"Just because."

Dora feels cornered.

"November fifth," she whispers.

Luka is silent. Maybe he's still doing the math. Then he breathes deeply. "I understand." His entire face lights up, and he grins with pleasure.

Dora doesn't reply. There's nothing to reply.

"I want to meet him."

So, here they are. She'd always been afraid of this.

Then, why is it that she feels so happy all of a sudden? As if she'd been set free?

Dora and Luka go walking. Along the beach. To the lighthouse. Then to the rock. But they stay on top of it, sit down on a stone. Luka puts his arm around Dora. It's cold and windy, and countless clouds scud past above them. The sea has grown wild. It snorts and whooshes and sprays, hurls itself tempestuously back and forth, like a caged beast. And as they raptly watch this performance, this battle, Luka tells the story of his second daughter, Maja, how she was conceived and came into the world, only one day after his son, and how seriously ill she was, and it makes Dora cry. And he tells her about his older daughter, Katja, who isn't even his daughter, but the result of a "slipup," as Klara called it, when he was in Paris and she was desperate, and she'd told Ana all about it, who confronted her right away, that's the way Ana is, because Luka hadn't spoken to her, not before and not since, absolutely never again. He knows the guy, though, he used to play water polo with him, and the guy donated a kidney for his daughter, and now Katja is healthy enough again to take care of her two little daughters, she's a great mother, a very good girl—young woman, that is—and she's achieved her dream of being a wonderful wife and mother, and again, Dora has to cry. When he tells her about his short career as a soldier, about his injury, and how Dora saved him, she bursts out crying yet again, because she remembers it, remembers his wound and the fear that took her breath away. And as he comes to the end of his story, he tells her of the day in the cellar, when he took out the pictures that have been painted since, about his decision to find Dora, to spend the rest of his life with his life, and then Dora cries even more, because she has waited for this moment her entire life, and now it's too late.

"Do you know what this whole story amounts to?"

"A surrealist horror show? Dalí at his peak?"

"A history of the countless pregnancies that changed the world."

Silence. Like gold. Followed by gales of tearful laughter.

"What now?"

"Let's get out of here."

Dora wipes away her tears and shakes her head.

"I can't. I'm married."

"But you love me!"

"Yes, I love you."

"Why did you marry him, then?" Luka doesn't even see how inappropriate his indignation is.

"He was there. He loves Nikola. Nikola likes him. He's good to me, and Nikola didn't want me to be alone when he goes off to sail the seas." Pause. "And sometimes I needed someone, too." Dora whispers this, as if she were embarrassed.

"How long have you been married?" Little by little his indignation turns into despair.

"Three years."

"What does he do?"

"He's a director. He's directed six of my plays."

"It's not that guy Frédéric, is it?!" Luka is getting angry. Standing up, he turns his back on her, concentrates on the roaring sea: a crazy south wind that thinks it's a hurricane.

"Of course not! His name is Roger."

"Roger? What kind of name is that?" Luka competes with the bellowing, salty churning water beneath him. "I hate him! God, how I hate him!"

Dora lets him vent his anger and disappointment and helplessness. And she tries to regain her own composure. Everything is in uproar.

"Where is he? Does he know that you're with me?"

"He and Nikola are in Split. I left them with a friendly actor I met at the festival in Avignon. I said, 'Let's visit good old Zlatko.' No, he doesn't know anything about you, he doesn't know that I'm with you. I just had the feeling, once again, that I had to see you, it was as if you had called me . . ." Dora trembles from the cold and from her emotions and from the cruel games of fate. Scraps of conversations she's had with different people about Luka and her over the years race through her head. She grows dizzy. Too many words. She feels the wind rustle her thoughts.

"I want you and my son, I want everything, finally, I have a right to it, I've waited so long that I've no longer even been waiting . . ." Luka starts counting. Dora stands up quickly and hugs him. And there they stand, like two tragic characters in a Shakespeare play. Like two lost children. Against the backdrop of nature's power.

"What do we do now?"

"Let's get out of here."

Acknowledgments

With all my heart I thank

Daša Dragnić, for her boundless support and for her unshakable belief in me;

Martin Hielscher, for his generous friendship;

Kristina Grasse, for all the encouraging phone calls and confidence-inspiring e-mails;

Karin Ertl, Kornelia Helfmann and Michael Kleinherne, for their probing questions;

Valérie Schüttler-Genetet and Manfred Gehrmann, my first readers;

Oliver Brauer, for his enthusiasm; and Marion Kohler and Britta Claus, who came to share it;

Eva and Lee Bacon, for being there for Dora and Luka when needed most; and Gesche Wendebourg for always knowing what to do;

Gregor, who shares my happiness and delights in it;

My Leon, for existing.